D. M. Greenwood has worked for twelve years in the
Diocese of Rochester as an ecclesiastical civil servant.
Her first degree was in Classics at Oxford and as a
mature student she took a second degree in Theology
at London University. She has also taught at a
number of schools, including St Paul's Girls' in
London. She lives overlooking the River Thames in
Greenwich, with her lurcher bitch.

Also by D. M. Greenwood

Clerical Errors
Unholy Ghosts
Idol Bones
Holy Terrors

Every Deadly Sin

D. M. Greenwood

HEADLINE

First published in 1995
by HEADLINE BOOK PUBLISHING

First published in paperback in 1995
by HEADLINE BOOK PUBLISHING

10 9 8 7 6 5 4 3 2 1

ISBN 0 7472 4984 9

Printed and bound in Great Britain by
Cox & Wyman Ltd, Reading, Berks

HEADLINE BOOK PUBLISHING
A division of Hodder Headline PLC
338 Euston Road
London NW1 3BH

For Keith Blackburn

Contents

CHAPTER ONE

Accidental Companions

Dead at last, thought Canon Beagle and read the obituary in the *Church Times* with delight. It ran:

> His many friends in many walks of church life will be saddened to learn of the death at the age of eighty-seven of Benjamin Derrick Tussock. Tusk, as he was known to his large acquaintance, was the son of a West Riding family whose father worked on the railway. He always said he had little early schooling but in 1933 he took up a place at Leeds University to study mechanical engineering.

Never knew that, thought Canon Beagle, chewing his teeth. Always reckoned Tussock was rather cack-handed in the practical area. Shows you can never tell. He pushed his glasses back up his long nose and pressed on with pleasure. In spite of his arthritis he felt all the well being which even the old living feel when contemplating the recent contemporary dead.

There he came under the influence of Chips Hollander, the university chaplain, to whose discerning eye the Anglican communion is indebted for many able clergy in the evangelical tradition. Chips used to boast that Tusk was his finest bag. Under Chips's aegis, Tusk went on to Oak Hill Theological College, and served his title at St Justus Without, Bradford. In 1940 he joined the Royal Marines and went through the war, first in the ranks and then as chaplain. In later years he used to say that the war made him. Certainly it gave him the opportunity to refine those pastoral and evangelical skills which were of such use to the Archdiocese of York when, in 1951, he became the Archbishop's Missioner at Large for the whole of the northern province. He threw himself with unexampled vigour into a task which, he always said, he thanked God, fitted him like a glove. There were few parishes which did not benefit from his unrivalled enthusiasm and unequalled skills.

'One way of putting it', Canon Beagle commented out loud. Others might have said no parish was free from his meddling. Teaching men twice his age how to run their parishes. He'd no shame, hadn't Tussock. No sense of the fitness of things. Old men don't like being told what to do by younger ones. Invigorated by his anger he scanned the final paragraphs.

These were years of Herculean effort for Tusk. He travelled widely over his huge cure; his sprightly figure and rubicund face with its famous smile were known both in the field and, if need be, in the corridors of power. Ever open to new ways of meeting and influencing people, he was one of the first among evangelicals to use retreat houses and pilgrimage centres as a way of spreading the faith and nurturing the Christian life in the post-war era. Many young people will recall with delight their first contact with the Church at Tusk's 'weekends' at St Sylvan's at Rest in the Yorkshire dales. His influence stretched well beyond the boundaries of parish or diocese. Intuitively he was able to meet the needs of his time; his little works on evangelism, *Fighting on Frontiers* and its successor *Knocking on Doors* were widely acclaimed. His preaching attracted large congregations in which members of the Government were often present. His opinion was sought by the media when the Church's views were required on the many ethical and political questions of our age. His pamphlets on the welfare state, homosexuality, free school meals and satanism were classics of their kind. Men of affairs respected him because, as he often told them, he was in touch with grass roots; clergy looked up to him because he had the ear of the great and the good.

For twenty years he bestrode the northern province like a Celtic saint of old. When he finally retired in 1989, he was made a residentiary Canon of Bow St Aelfric where, in spite of increasing deafness, he carried on a wide-ranging ministry. He died, as he would have wished, in collar. His was a very public life. His was a prophetic voice. We thank God for it. His loyal wife of fifty-seven years, Muriel, his strength and stay, as he used to call her, survives him.

Canon Beagle savoured the heartiness, the cosiness of it all. The mind of the *Church Times* at its flabby best. Unequalled this, unrivalled that. Who'd written the thing? Pity they'd not asked him. He could a tale unfold. 'Like a Celtic saint', forsooth. How we love to trick out our tiny efforts in ancient vestments. 'A public life.' A whitened sepulchre more like. 'A prophetic voice.' The clergy always speak of the prophetic voice when one of their number had meddled in politics instead of keeping to his altar and office. Canon Beagle felt his blood pressure throb in his temples.

About St Sylvan's though, he had to admit, they were dead right; he'd done a lot for the place; he'd had an eye to the main, the fashionable, chance had Tusk. Canon Beagle put the paper down on his lap and surveyed the long, narrow drawing-room of the Bishop Herbert Residential Nursing Home for Retired Clergy and their Relicts in what was once a fashionable suburb of Leeds. This time next week, he thought, I'll be there. I'll be free of this damned prison. St Sylvan's waits for me. I can't now be far from death. I must make one more effort to learn what I ought to know. I'll get there if it kills me. Just for one last go. To set the record straight.

He glanced with distaste at the pair of young, how young, auxiliary nurses who were propelling Muriel Tussock towards the television room. The screen was showing a rugby international to an audience of five old women. Fat lot Muriel'd get out of it; she'd had Alzheimer's for three years. Did she know, Canon Beagle wondered, that she was at last free of her husband?

'Come on, love, your turn now,' said the younger of the auxiliaries descending on him.

'Don't,' began Canon Beagle peremptorily.

'You'll like it,' she assured him and then resumed her conversation with her companion.

'She had to have him put down in the end.'

Canon Beagle froze.

'He lost his teeth. It was all that soft food and he used to be ever so partial to a bone.'

'God help me,' the Canon prayed.

'My aunty's went the same way,' said her companion. 'It was only a mongrel, though. Hold tight, love,' she said, tucking the Canon's rug over his knees and releasing the brake on his wheelchair. They made for the front row of the television room at a cracking pace.

Canon Tussock's death was remarked and, in its way, celebrated in a number of households. At eight-thirty a.m. in Tunbridge Wells, for example, Mrs Lemming tugged the drawstring, drew back the dining-room curtains and looked out on to the tiny garden of the Edwardian villa. The garden, no bigger than the dining-room in which she stood, was just as well appointed. The early morning sun of a fine July day filtered through the foliage of the wych-hazel but hesitated, as though uncertain of its welcome, to enter the room. This time next week, Mrs Lemming thought, I shall be in Yorkshire. I shall be at St Sylvan's. I shall be free. It will all be much better.

Since his retirement, the Reverend Norman Lemming had taken to reading the obituaries first, not because his acquaintance were dying at a faster pace than previously but because Lemming felt that they should be. Now he had ceased to be the incumbent of St Justus by the Well, a limbo which felt very like death, he could see no reason why the Church should continue to exist. In his heart he had always supposed that the Second Coming would occur before he retired so that he would, as it were, be taken up in his full professional glory.

He cleared his throat in a mild, purposeful way, which Mrs Lemming had learned was intended to make her pay attention. She continued to gaze at the white lilies round the bole of the wych-hazel. Her own name was Hazel. She felt an affinity with the tree. Norman cleared his throat again, more loudly, and creaked in his chair. More concerned to prevent his moving too strenuously in the antique piece than to comply with his request for her notice, she returned to the breakfast table and attacked an egg.

'Of course, he was never a first-rate scholar, more a populariser, but eighty-seven is no great age nowadays. I well remember . . .'

'Who?'

'Ben Tussock. Tusk.'

'Who?' Mrs Lemming no longer bothered to restrain her hostility to her husband. She was, in fact, unsure whether she was slightly deaf but, when conversing with Norman, she had resolved to give herself the benefit of the doubt.

'Canon Tussock. Yorkshireman. I, of course, used to know him when he was getting St Sylvan's into shape. But you may have met him at a garden party at Emma.'

'What?'

'Cambridge. Emmanuel College. Garden party. Festival of Britain year or thereabouts.'

'How did he die?' asked Mrs Lemming, cutting through several stages in the conversation which her husband would have preferred to go through one by one; undergraduate days of modest success, a college chaplaincy just missed, distinguished contemporaries. He was aware of being cheated.

'I well remember . . .'

'Have you finished with the marmalade?'

He nudged the cut-glass dish with its pale-yellow burden across the table. His wife watched his arthritic hand cupped awkwardly against the edge of the bowl. As though it had no sensitivity at all, she thought without pity. She split her toast exactly in two.

'He spat when he talked,' she said. 'And he talked a lot. Little Shavian man. Lot of energy.'

If occasionally his own talent for deflation was anticipated and surpassed by his wife's, Lemming never allowed her to suppose it. He switched now with practised ease to new ground.

'An enormously valuable contribution,' he said reverently.

'To what?'

'He helped to bring in the Kingdom.'

In all her thirty years of marriage Hazel Lemming had never found a way of dealing with this particular move. In youth straightforward piety had prevented her meeting it head-on. She had thought, in her innocence, that life with Norman would reveal what counted as 'the Kingdom'. But, as the years passed, she had grown no wiser and had in time come to feel that there was no life in the phrase, not merely for her but (and this had shaken her to despair) for Norman too. It had been merely one of many counters in the game whereby Norman brought the recalcitrant to heel. The children had suffered it for as long as they had to and then, as soon as it became economically possible, had quietly deserted for Yorkshire and America. She herself had genuinely struggled for a number of years to learn the language of her husband's religion. It was, after all, his overt piety and the learning which, she assumed, supported it, that had attracted her to him when he'd come as a curate to her parents' parish. She had wanted (*he* had been happy that *she* had wanted) to be his pupil. But as she had reached middle age, it seemed less and less that Norman's language illuminated her own fraught experience. In the end she'd given up trying to understand it, though the guilt of failure haunted her and afforded (she was aware) a foothold for Norman's capacity for blame.

'Lucky old man,' she said.
'What?'
'Tussock. Lucky to be dead.'

'You can tell what the grub's going to be like by the marmalade.'

The Reverend Theodora Braithwaite, a woman of about thirty in Anglican deacons' orders, who felt that conversation at breakfast was to be deprecated, mumbled in the hope that no more would follow. The high-ceilinged college dining-hall was, at this early morning hour, only lightly littered with breakfasters all widely dispersed over the large area. She had expected to be able to eat undisturbed.

'I was at Keele last year and it was pale yellow with very thin peel. No use to man or beast.'

'Ah.'

'The year before that, that's my first year, I was at UEA and they didn't have marmalade at all, just plastic individualised miniatures of jam.'

'Uh-huh?'

'This isn't bad.' He prodded it with a fork. 'Got a bit of body to it.'

In despair Theodora raised her eyes from her letter and glanced at the thin boy opposite her. He was pale, with mousey hair cut in a fringe. His eyes were bright grey and active like those of a small mammal, a vole or a water rat. They gave him the air of something sprightly and intelligent which had to be constantly alert to avoid a predator. Whose food was he? Theodora wondered.

9

He had no visible beard. He was dressed, as many Open University students were, as though for a day's rock-climbing, with heavy boots, padded red nylon anorak and a red wooly hat with a bobble on it tucked into his shoulder strap.

'So you're going to be all right this time?'

'Reckon so. Even if the teaching's poor, it's not too much of a waste if the grub's good.'

'Are they connected?'

'What? Oh, food and education. Well, yes. I think so. Healthy mind, healthy body like. You learn better if you're properly fed, so you probably teach better if you're properly fed too.'

Theodora perceived only a tenuous connection. At both Cheltenham and Oxford the food had been vile but both teaching and learning of a high order.

'What are you reading?'

'Reading? I've got a *Guardian* if you want to ... Oh, I see what you ... Studying. Here. Well, I'm on my last now. Level three for honours. British empiricists.'

'How's it going?'

'I can manage Locke. Berkeley seems to me to be a nutter. Hume I can't get the hang of at all. I can't tell when he's serious or whether he's simply joking. "Reason is and ought only to be the slave of the passions." I hope someone's going to enlighten me this week.'

Theodora wondered to which of her colleagues on the Open University staff it would fall to take this young man through the elaborate embroidery of Hume's irony.

'What are you studying? Reading?' asked the young man, alive to his social duties.

'Teaching,' said Theodora. 'Level three. British empiri-cists.' She gave him a hard look.

'That's good. Just what I need. Know anything about Hume?'

'Yes.'

'Well, I hope I'm in your group then,' said the boy in the tone of one who intends to get his money's worth. It was a tone which Theodora had met before among Open University students who were paying their own fees and one of which, on the whole, she approved.

'That would be nice. However, if you'll excuse me?' She indicated the letter which lay beside her plate.

'Yes. Sorry. Go ahead.' The youth seemed content to return to his marmalade.

Theodora drew out the thin pages covered with neat spiky script and looked once more at the relevant pas-sage. 'Your godmother will want to see you since you're so rarely in the North. I said you'd ring her sometime before you go to St Sylvan's. I trust I have your move-ments correct?' You bet he did, thought Theodora. 'It's especially important, I feel, and I'm sure you share my feelings, to get in touch with her in the light of Ben Tussock's demise. They were very old friends and I expect she will feel the loss. It will make an enormous difference to Guy if he gets the money, as I suppose he might. Though given how much Ben disliked his son perhaps we should not prophesy about his attitude to his grandson. I hardly see why they should need an inquest given his age. It must be distressing for his widow, though I seem to remember that Muriel has gone into a nursing home, so perhaps she's past caring. I would hope in due course to have word of you (which I do not seem to have had for some considerable time) if your duties at your new university allow you a moment. I enclose, in case you should have missed it, the obituary from the *Church Times*. I am your affectionate uncle, Hugh Braithwaite.'

Theodora considered this harpoon from all angles. Her dead father's uncle, Canon Hugh Braithwaite, now retired to a fenland retreat, kept up a brisk correspondence with the younger members of the family, brisker indeed than some of them, with careers to make and less leisure than the Canon, could cope with. However, he was right and she ought to have written. He should have a card. She'd send him one from St Sylvan's when she got there next Saturday.

She read the obituary with pleasure. She remembered Tussock. He'd come down to Cheltenham in her last year to present the prizes. The obituary, she felt, captured the man in every bogus nuance; a pretend scholar, an imitation gentleman, a clerical counterpart of Shaw; jaunty, claiming, an enamoured spectator of his own surprising success. The Church, which so often in its upper echelons provides security for the only lightly endowed, had done well by Tusk. He had hit the moment and, not without skill, had adapted his person to the Church's needs. There had been a time when he was scarcely ever off the radio or television, pontificating on this and that. Many among the clergy had apparently felt that he could understand the contemporary world and interpret it to them. Theodora, as the eighth generation of her family in clerical (albeit, in her case, deacons') orders, had noticed that the Church very often needs to have its own version of whatever the secular world is worshipping at any given moment. Tusk had fitted the bill for the age of the instant expert. He had been able to reassure clergy that they too could produce, in response to modern agendas, modern thinkers who were also practical men of the world. If it turned out that in the process of interpretation the great spiritual truths of Christianity had been lost or deformed and all that remained was rhetoric or journalism, by the time that was generally apparent, the audience was, as often as not, dead – like Tusk.

Theodora raised her eyes from the letter and gazed round the dining-hall. She was here for a week to earn a little spare cash by teaching at the Open University summer school. As the regular students flooded out for the vacation, the Open University moved in and swiftly remade the institution in its own energetic image. Blue-and-white notices flaunting the OU logo directed the temporary staff to one set of facilities and temporary students to another. People walked fast and talked hard as though they had long been denied that delight. Students had this one week in a year's study to sample the pleasures of residence. They were, most of them, determined to wring the last drop from the experience. Theodora, on leave from her curacy in a South London parish, loved the buzz, the concentration, the eager intellectual need and diversity of the students. Cynicism was absent, engagement apparent on all sides. As she'd collected her toast and coffee from the servery, she'd overheard two ladies of advanced years discussing with equal knowledge and no distinction in tone the quality of the bacon and the success of Henry James's narrative techniques. Theodora loved them deeply.

The university building in which they were located for this year's effort resembled a lake dwellers' settlement. Colleges, a library and an administrative block had been constructed on an imperfectly drained marsh connected by a string of long shallow lakes. The buildings were without distinction, flimsy and beginning to corrode in vital places now, thirty years after their erection. But the idiosyncrasy of the site remained and charmed. Mallard of immense girth with the odd smiling Aylesbury decorated the lakes. Stepping-stones sunk in the water connecting the back doors of the colleges provided a tiny adventure when seeking access to classes. There was a toyishness, a humour almost, about the settlement which communicated itself both to staff (porters were civil) and students. For the last two years Theodora had done a week here in the summer, teaching one of the philosophy courses. She always enjoyed it. On this her first morning, however, the wind was battering at the wall of glass which formed on one side of the dining-hall, tossing rain and spray from the fountain in the middle of the largest lake. Wherever her first class was (she had yet to find out where that might be) she would get wet going to it.

'It's going to be wet.'

Theodora looked across at the young man, surprised to find him still there.

'I've got an umbrella if you'd care to share it.' His

accent, she noticed, was northern without being over-bearingly so.

Theodora peered at the label on the young man's anorak. She could just make out the name. 'Guy Tussock.'

'Are we going in the same direction?' Theodora enquired.

'I'm sure I am,' answered the young man courteously.

CHAPTER TWO

St Sylvan's at Rest

The shrine of St Sylvan at Rest in North Yorkshire is a comparatively recent addition to the pilgrimage places of the Anglican communion. It was discovered in the 1930s in the days before the Second World War. It became and has remained a place of pilgrimage for the discerning for half a century.

The discovery and sponsoring of the shrine was the work of a remarkable man. The Reverend Augustine Bellaire was not perhaps entirely orthodox in every respect. Certainly he allowed himself to invent tradition when he felt the greater good was so served. In his own person too there was flamboyance which some found difficult to tolerate. His taste in clerical dress ran to the colourful and, his enemies had it, popish. He was invariably accompanied by a pair of large deer-hounds which went with him into chapel at St Sylvan's and slept under the pulpit. He had a fine tenor voice and was inclined to sing the entire liturgy unaided and unaccompanied. As age advanced he became unpredictable and suffered, it was observed, from violent swings of mood. He would allow no vehicles within two miles of St Sylvan's and there was neither television, wireless nor newspapers in the guest-house. He died in 1988 but his spirit hovered yet, so his friends asserted, over the place he had loved.

What he did not invent, since it is recorded in Bede's *Historia Ecclesiastica Gentis Anglorum*, was the legend of St Sylvan himself. The saint, Bede tells us, was originally a Roman Army officer, Titus Sylvanus Aurelianus, hailing from the region we now think of as Poland. He served in the cavalry attached to the Ninth Legion stationed, in AD 400, at Eboracum, later, of course, York. In the course of a deer hunt Sylvanus's closest comrade was killed by an arrow shot from the bow of a fellow huntsman. Whilst mourning his loss, Sylvanus became acquainted with the Christian faith which held out the promise of resurrection and a future life. Much attracted by this teaching and reassured thereby that he would meet his friend in a nobler and more glorious sphere, he converted to the faith and was baptised in the baptistry of St Peter's York in 403.

Thus far the historian. Legend takes up the narrative. Sylvanus felt his previous martial calling to be incompatible with his new faith. He resigned his commission and took land near Rest, Castra Renastarum, forty miles east of York, in country well known for the excellence of its hunting forests. There he lived peacably enough in those troubled times which followed the withdrawal of the Roman Army from Britain, farming his acres like many another until the Pictish invasion of 435. In that year, confronted one warm July night by an enemy raiding party, he was forced once more to take up the sword to defend his house and family. Though he fought with his ancient courage, as the story has it, in the end the pagan horde prevailed. He saw his house and barns torched and witnessed the slaughter of his wife and sons. He himself was captured and, even as he invoked the power of Christ and his saints, flung into his own well where he died with the Saviour's name upon his lips. Whether he was ever regularly canonised is obscure. Local pride, however, chose to bestow the style of saint upon him. For a thousand years he was honoured in folklore. His well, a place of modest pilgrimage, was yearly dressed on the day of his martrydom, 25 July, by the neighbouring villagers with the locally named herb-Sylvane, a botanical relation of herb-Robert, which flourished in the surrounding woodland. The Reformation put an end to such pieties and for another four hundred years his name was recorded only on maps in the form of St Sylvan's well. Later still even the exact location of the well was lost to human knowledge.

In the late summer of 1937, however, Augustine Bellaire, then a young undergraduate fresh from his studies at Oxford and much inspired by stories of the English saints and martyrs retailed to him by his Anglo-Catholic tutors, took it into his head to seek out the site of the ancient martyrdom of St Sylvan. Augustine was staying at the time at Broadcourt, the manor of Sir Lucius Broad, on whose land the putative well of St Sylvan stood. It was, in truth, no great task of scholarship to retrieve from the records in Sir Lucius's library the probable location of the well. Accordingly one hot July morning after a night of heavy rain, Augustine strode out early, a panama hat upon his head, his Oxford bags flapping, his Lancing first eleven tie holding them up, a canvas knapsack on his shoulder, in the direction in which his researches had indicated the well might be found.

In high hopes and at a swinging pace he struck out along a rutted sheep track between thyme-covered banks towards the higher woodland in which he expected to make his discovery. Augustine, however, was reading theology, not geography. By early afternoon he was thoroughly lost. He lay down in the shade of an oak tree to refresh himself on the ham sandwiches thoughtfully provided by his host's housekeeper and after his repast fell, in the manner of youth, into a deep sleep. When he awoke the sun was declining and the light fading. Alarmed, not indeed for his own safety, but for the anxiety which his absence might occasion in his host, he hastened to take his bearings and retrace his steps. The appearance of a short cut lured him in the time-honoured fashion of fairytale until, at last, he found himself scrambling amidst rocks steeper than those he had hitherto encountered. It was, therefore, with relief that he raised his head from his exertions to see flickering, as it seemed not too far ahead and below him, a light which must surely betoken habitation and help. But as he slithered and stumbled downhill the ground suddenly opened at his feet. In vain did he clasp at the trunk of an attendant ilex, for, in a trice he was precipitated into a shallow chasm.

When he recovered, he found himself standing on the brink of a pool about twenty yards across, the edges of which were banked in places with stones cut in an antique mode. closely fitting to each other without mortar. The surface of the pool was motionless, though his ear detected the sound of water splashing and bubbling close at hand, the origin of which he could not, though he looked about him, discover.

The quietness, the solitude of the place in the gathering darkness moved him greatly. Almost as in a ritual, murmuring a grace, he knelt down, cupped his hands and drank from the water. Even as he did so, he felt a sudden cooling of the temperature. About what happened next he refused always thereafter to speak. Suffice it to say that he fell into a faint and when he came to in the warmth of the early morning sun, the first thing which his eye lighted upon was the head of a deer carved in stone surmounted by a plaque on which was inscribed in Roman capitals '*QUI RESTITIT EI PAX DATUR*'. As Augustine gazed into the calm, innocent eyes of the hind, he vowed that St Sylvan's well, for such it must surely be, should become for others a place of refreshment and revelation as it had been for him.

Half a century after its discovery by Bellaire, the shrine of St Sylvan, when the summer mist veiled it in early morning, looked almost respectably ancient. The small spire on top of the squat tower of the chapel could have been mediaeval. The farmhouse and its kitchen, a light from which had enticed Bellaire on the night of his discovery, had been enlarged with accommodation for pilgrims. This guest-house, the modernity of which nothing could disguise, was modestly hidden under flowering creepers. Next to both guest-house and kitchen was a walled garden, planted to suggest a greater age than it in fact possessed, where pilgrims could walk and meditate. Thought had been taken to link buildings as well as life with the past. A path to the holy well wound from the west door of the chapel and disappeared as the terrain grew steeper. Behind the buildings the wooded hills rose in a defending circle. At this time of day (it was as yet still early in the morning) there was no traffic on the narrow road which mounted the hillside to within a couple of miles of the small paradise which Father Bellaire had created.

In the garden Ruth Swallow surveyed the rows of broad beans. Gently she lifted a pod and rubbed her thumb down it. It came away black and sticky with fly. The sweat broke on her brow and she caught her breath as the sickness gripped her. The heat came in waves from the high stone walls. For a moment the branches of the espaliered fruit trees seemed to lurch towards her as though they would entangle her in their net. The huge mulberry tree in the centre of the garden seemed to expand to the size of a mountain and reared up as though it might fall upon her. She pushed her hands down her hips and steadied herself. She looked towards the chapel spire and made out the gilded hands of the clock. Six-thirty. They were due in twelve hours. She felt a surge of emotion, fear and hope mixed. Let the beans wait. She had had to wait.

Inside the guest-house, in the office which looked out on the garden, Tom Bough whistled through his teeth, like an ostler, his dad always said. Tom didn't know what an ostler was but inferred it might be some sort of musi-cal instrument of the kind which the old man had slung up on the wall of that noisome den in which he squatted. Anyway, he didn't care enough to ask.

On the desk which he was dusting, was a list in com-puter script which bore today's date, Saturday, 19 July. Tom ran his eye down it. The Revd Canon H. Beagle. He'd heard his dad mention him. He'd been before. Some time ago though. Ex-athlete, big fellow with arthritis. The Revd T. Braithwaite. Who was he? Familiar name but couldn't place him. Mr and Mrs V. Clutton Brock. Didn't know them either. Mrs Lemming. Lemming, that would be Nor-man's wife or perhaps his widow. Terrible little man, Norman Lemming, pal of Tusk's. Tunbridge Wells some-where. Mr Guy Tussock. Tussock, now that *was* a well-known name. So he'd decided to come, had he?

In two parallel columns were the room numbers of the guests and their dietary requirements. Beagle and Braithwaite both had an A beside them to betoken that they ate anything. Mr Guy Tussock was awarded a VFE for vegetarian who ate fish and eggs. Mr Clutton Brock had a G beside him which meant gluten free (he'd be a right pain). Mrs C.B. was a V for vegan, no fish or eggs. Beside Mrs Lemming nothing was recorded. At the bottom of the page after the word 'Director' had been pencilled in the Revd A. Bootle. They must be middle-of-the-roaders then, neither high- nor low-Church if Angus was in charge of them. Either that or he was the only one they could get to come in. Which was likely enough in the present state of play.

Tom lifted the page of the flimsy paper taking care that his dirty thumb should leave no trace on its surface and glanced at the list underneath. It bore the date of the next day, Sunday the twentieth. Yes, there it was, the second, non-residential party, just as Ruth had said. The Rt. Revd Francis Peake, the Ven. Jonathan Gosh and the Revd the Hon. Martha Broad. All had As beside them. Capable of devouring any flesh, Ruth had said. Come to gobble us up, they have. So it wouldn't be long now before they knew their fate, whether they were to live or die.

In the distance he heard a door open. He took his eye off the list and slowly polished his way round the desk. Brass pen tray to the left, dust; brass pen tray to the right, dust. Brass crucifix, ditto. He resumed his hissing as a commentary on his actions. His eye followed his hand. His words preceded his thoughts. Let them come, he muttered to himself. He raised his eyes to the wall behind the desk. 'They that wait upon the Lord shall renew their strength.' Isaiah. Well, he thought, we shall see. I've done a lot of waiting after all. Time my strength was renewed.

'Where are we?' Mrs Lemming enquired fretfully.

The only answer was the clash of the minibus's gears and the clanking of the exhaust pipe against its undercarriage, as it ground its way through the late afternoon football traffic of the first of the pre-season friendlies. They seemed to have made no progress for hours. Mrs Lemming, on the front seat behind the driver, bumped and swayed on the sagging upholstery. It was possible the driver hadn't heard her. It was possible he did not know. Perhaps he simply didn't think she was worth answering. Mrs Lemming had often evoked the latter response. She knew she wasn't worth bothering with; Norman had taught her. I'd hoped for better, she thought. It's got to be better than this.

The only other passengers were a middle-aged couple they had picked up at Bradford Station. They sat on the back seat barricaded behind their luggage which was plentiful, in matching tartan suitcases of various sizes. Propped on the seat in front of them was an enormous black case the shape of a cello. Whenever the bus changed gear it bucked forward as though it had a life of its own. They had spoken no word either to her or to each other as they had lurched and stumbled down the centre gangway.

Were they stunned from the train journey? Mrs Lemming wondered. She herself had made Doncaster in reasonably good order from Tunbridge Wells an hour ahead of them. She had spotted the bus marked 'St Sylvan's at Rest' in hand-painted blue letters on the flaking white paint and deposited her own more modest collection of bags on the rack above her seat. On the bench beside her she propped the easel which she had packed so carefully and so surreptitiously. Even so, she hadn't escaped Norman's notice. 'A pilgrimage, a retreat,' he'd said, 'isn't a holiday. I think you will find that St Sylvan's ... though of course without Ben ...' He'd trailed off defeated by mortality, then returned to the attack with new vigour. 'I doubt if you'll need that.' But she'd stood her ground. She'd resisted in her evasive way. 'I expect you're right, but you never know.' And before he could object further she had pressed it into the taxi-driver's hands and doubled into the cab after it. There, she thought, as she hugged it to her, my pilgrimage has almost begun.

The bus lurched forward after its considerable pause and she leaned her head against the cool dirty glass of the window. Traffic stretched as far as her eye could see through a haze of exhaust fumes hanging in the hot air. Away to the right she could just make out a signpost: 'Leeds Central'. They were doing, like the stations of the cross, a tour of the railway stations of the West Riding. The information leaflet had said – she searched in her bag – 'Our bus will take you from your station to St Sylvan's.' But it wasn't taking them to St Sylvan's. Any-where but. Perhaps we'll never get there. Perhaps we'll just go on driving from station to station in this excruciat-ing heat for ever. She felt near to tears.

To steady herself she looked at the driver. She could see his back clad in a grey flannel shirt through which the sweat showed in dark patches on his shoulder blades. Rising out of the crumpled collar was an inch or two of stubble-like bristle, so sharp that it looked dangerous.

Above it a strong growth of grey clotted hair mounted up the cranium like a crop on a hillside. If she looked in his driving mirror she could see a reflection of the front of him. The bristles of his beard went a long way down his neck and disappeared into a matted growth visible on his chest through his unbuttoned shirt. He is not my idea of a pilgrimage leader, Mrs Lemming from Tunbridge Wells thought.

At Leeds Station, Canon Beagle manoeuvred his wheelchair up and down the parking area, scattering pedestrians in his path. He had made no apology. When his arthritis had finally prevailed and he'd been reduced to a chair, he'd resolved he'd make no concessions. He'd go on just as he always had. He liked a challenge. He particularly liked signs which said 'No Disabled Access'. His greatest feat to date, he reckoned, had been the steps of the Athenaeum. He'd commandeered two well-built archdeacons and blackmailed them of their Christian charity to take a wheel each and heave him up. He was helping them to keep fit, he reckoned. So now he rolled up and down the indeterminate area between the taxi ranks and the station booking-office, twenty yards each way and then the equivalent of a handbrake turn and back again. He'd just accomplished the ninth of these when he spotted the St Sylvan's bus nosing its way through the cabs. He remarked with pleasure the narrow door and steep steps of the minibus's entrance. She'd be a poser.

The hirsute driver swung himself down from the driving seat and surveyed the wheelchair. He eyed Canon

Beagle as an adversarial equal. He said nothing but weighed up the distances silently for a moment then, with a swift movement, he seized the handles of the chair, tipped it slightly backward until the feet pedals rested on the bottom step of the bus and then with a jerk heaved the whole through the door. Canon Beagle, no bantamweight, was impressed. The driver slewed the chair round and locked it into a couple of floor bolts designed to hold it.

The driver eased himself back behind the wheel. They were all set then, thought Mrs Lemming, who had remarked Canon Beagle's clerical collar and felt that in some way its presence marked the proper beginning of the pilgrimage. The driver revved the engine and let in the clutch. Then he stamped on his brake. Something was happening outside the bus in front of them. A high boyish voice could be heard clamouring outside in the street. 'Hang on. Half a mo,' it said. Mrs Lemming crouched forward to get a look. Jumping up and down in front of the bus was a small figure in a red-and-white-check shirt and shiny black nylon cycling pants which stopped just above the knee. The boy was steadying a yellow mountain bike in his right hand and his left held a red nylon knapsack. On his head was a red knitted cap. The driver wound down the window.

'St Sylvan's?' said the figure. 'Guy Tussock,' it added. 'Can I put my bike in the boot?'

'No boot,' said the driver with satisfaction.

'Well actually it folds up.' Guy bent round his bicycle, twiddled a couple of bolts and the bike folded neatly in

28

upon itself, wheel to wheel. Reluctantly the driver admitted defeat. The door was opened and Guy manoeuvred his machine aboard. Once it had been stowed behind the driver and in front of the flinching Mrs Lemming, Guy slid himself into a seat in front of the Clutton Brocks, breathed in and out six times, folded his legs into a good full lotus, placed his hands on each bare knee and closed his eyes. He clearly had his methods of dealing with boring journeys.

The driver too had his methods of passing the time. As he achieved the highest gear he leaned forward in the driving seat, fiddled for a moment and then switched on the radio. The thud of heavy metal shook the small space. Canon Beagle was aware of a twittering protest stemming from behind his right ear but the angle of his chair was such that he couldn't turn round. He bethought him of the driver's interior mirror and focused his gaze on the reflection. Mrs Lemming could be seen making small signals of distress. Behind her, on the back seat, he glimpsed a tubby man caught with a look of horror on his features and a hard-boiled egg held in his hand at chin-level. His eyes bulged with shock as the drums got to him. Canon Beagle watched with interest as the man took a napkin from his knee and heaved himself out of his seat. The vehicle picked up speed as it left the traffic of Leeds behind. Mr Clutton Brock swayed his way down the central aisle. Canon Beagle watched the reflection turning into reality as he hoved abreast of the wheelchair.

The man was fiftyish, dressed in a green tweed suit.

His thin fair hair was economically arranged across his pate. He bent his head down just behind the driver's ear, steadied himself with his free hand and kept the egg clear of the driver's cheek. Then he shouted in a high, penetrating voice, 'It may have escaped your notice but we consider ourselves to be on a pilgrimage. Would you mind turning that thing off?'

The driver gave no sign of having heard him. Then, his eye still entirely concentrated on the road, he flicked the switch. The throb of the engine felt like silence. The pilgrim executed a three-point turn, guarding his egg the while, and started back towards the rear. He had reached halfway when the music blared forth again. The man flushed purple, stopped and started to turn round. The bus heeled over to cope with a corner and the man was flung into a vacant seat. As he rose again and struggled to start forward, the driver flicked the switch and once again quiet returned. The man hesitated for a moment, threw a baffled look at the driver and then picked his way back to his seat.

Theodora, boarding the bus at York station forty minutes later, scented the turbulence. All is not well, she thought, scanning the tense faces with a skilled pastoral eye. She'd better see what she could do. Who looked most in need? It was a toss-up between the woman in the purple cardigan just behind the driver and the old cleric in the wheelchair, his hands clamped on his panama hat. The couple in the rear had, after all, each other. Guy's neat figure, deep in the fissure between the middle seats, she did not detect. Providence decided for her. The driver let in the clutch suddenly and the vehicle jumped forward precipitating her into the seat beside the wheelchair.

The Canon turned a concerned face towards her. 'I hope you're all right. These physical surprises can be painful.'

Theodora regained her breath and nodded. 'Fine, thank you.' She saw a large head in the mode of a Roman senator. It had a strong nose, thin lips and a growth of thick curly grey hair which did credit to a man who must be in his eighties. A connoisseur in the genre, she took in the excellence of his clerical suiting.

'I'm Canon Henry Beagle. And you would be?'

'Theodora Braithwaite.'

'Ah. Braithwaite. A clerical name. I wonder, would you by any chance be any relation of Nicholas?'

'My father.' Theodora embarked on the familiar catechism.

'I was so sorry to hear of his early death. A remarkable man.'

'Yes, he was. So do I. Miss him, I mean.'

'And Canon Hugh, of course . . .'

'My great uncle.'

'A distinguished family.'

'So far,' Theodora deprecated.

'But you carry on the tradition?'

'I'm in deacons' orders, yes,' Theodora admitted.

There was a slight pause and then Canon Beagle's curiosity got the better of his good manners. 'Will you seek priests' orders?' he enquired.

'No. Not until the whole Church has made up its mind on the matter. There's very little that I can do, that needs to be done, that can't be done as a deacon. The priest thing seems rather too closely connected with wanting power. Best left, I've come to feel.'

Canon Beagle felt this was all he could desire. He folded his arthritic hands with their enlarged knuckles on his broad chest and prepared to give himself up to the pleasures of clerical conversation with a sympathetic companion. Outside the window of the minibus, the plain of Yorkshire sped past disclosing fields of mown barley, the stubble bleached by the July sun. The bus's engine ceased to complain and settled into a steady low roar.

'Where would you be serving at the moment?' Canon Beagle pursued. 'A chaplaincy perhaps?' He could imagine Theodora in a hospital. She looked competent, a list-maker, if he were not mistaken. A good woman at a death-bed, he wouldn't be surprised, like Mrs Gaskell.

'I did a first curacy in East Africa. Now I'm doing a second at St Sylvester's Betterhouse in South London.'

'Ah. St Sylvester's. Gilbert Racy, Geoffrey Brighouse. Very interesting area.' Canon Beagle positively purred. He knew them both. The ecclesiastical pedigree could not have been better.

'St Sylvan's at Rest,' he said, 'have you been there before?'

Theodora shook her head. 'No. My uncle Hugh recommended it as a complete change from London and as I was in the North anyway, it seemed worth making the effort. I have to admit I've never made a pilgrimage.'

'Never done the Walsingham run?' Canon Beagle showed surprise.

'No, nor the Glastonbury one either.'

'Glastonbury's difficult,' said Canon Beagle, a connoisseur of these matters. 'The pagan associations are so strong there, one can waste an awful lot of time repelling the Arthurian brigade or the Wikke element. Purity's very important. We've simply got to draw the line somewhere.'

Theodora wasn't entirely convinced of this. She felt pilgrimages, like the Church, should be capacious. A gaggle of true believers reinforcing each other's bigotries might not be the best setting for revelation or even, more modestly, new learning.

'I've spent time at Little Gidding,' Theodora said, not wishing to disappoint him.

'It has its strengths,' Canon Beagle conceded. 'But it's very different from St Sylvan's which has a flavour all of its own. Little Gidding concentrates on the Christian life, St Sylvan's tends to have its focus on the well, naturally. Water does draw us, don't you find?'

Theodora agreed. 'We hope to be clean, new made over.'

'Quite so. And of course in my own case, it takes away my weight and frees me from my body. An analogue of Heaven, perfection.'

'What's St Sylvan's like? No pagan associations?'

'All the best sites have an atmosphere and there's no doubt that the more ancient, the more saturated in prayer, the more potent to move us.'

'Magic?' Theodora hazarded.

'Numinous,' Canon Beagle corrected her.

'The legend of St Sylvan,' Theodora was hesitant, 'it resonances of the Old English legends. Herne the Hunter. Slaying of the innocent. That sort of thing.'

Canon Beagle was unmoved. 'No doubt. I've always thought that the very best religious stories start in myth which is universal and then end up being incarnated in religious truth, Christian truth, which is historical, concrete and particular.'

'And Father Bellaire?'

Canon Beagle grinned, 'Kept deer-hounds.'

'You knew him well?'

Canon Beagle pursed his lips. 'On and off. I used to go regularly when I was home on leave from China and before Tusk got hold of the place.'

'Cannon Tussock was a rather different kettle of fish?'

'I've no doubt the evangelical wing meets many needs,' said Canon Beagle with distaste.

'I suppose people look for different things from a pilgrimage,' Theodora advanced cautiously.

'What would you be looking for in this pilgrimage?' Canon Beagle asked, suddenly direct. It was the tone, Theodora recognised it instantly, of someone who had years of experience in the field, who was in fact an authority.

Theodora considered his question. There were matters with which it would be tiresome to burden Canon Beagle. Emotions, relationships were not the fodder of casual acquaintance. It wasn't the confessional, telling all was not required. She selected. 'I suppose if I'm honest I'm looking for a way to reunite the different bits of me. My work, I mean in Betterhouse, it's, well, it's diverse and draining. We see a lot of people in trouble so dire they can't rise out of it and violence is often the only way they have to express themselves.'

'It's contagious, violence. It draws other people in and goes on down the generations so it becomes an institution. It's very difficult to break it. Perhaps only a saint can manage it.' Canon Beagle had not, after all, led a sheltered life, Theodora surmised.

As he finished speaking, Mrs Lemming leaned across the aisle from her seat. Their conversation had not been conducted in whispers. The noise of the engine had made them speak more loudly than they had realised.

'I do so agree with you,' she said rapidly. 'I mean about evil being contagious, drawing you in so that you get sucked down into someone else's whirlpool. Wouldn't you say that marriage was a bit like that?' She appealed first to Canon Beagle then Theodora.

Theodora felt her own inadequacy. She hesitated. Canon Beagle turned a gentle eye to the little cardiganed figure who, in her agitation, had clutched her easel to her as though for comfort. 'I've often seen it,' he assured her.

Mrs Lemming pressed on as though she hadn't heard him. 'I live in Tunbridge Wells. I'm making a pilgrimage to find somewhere to start from. I want a birth, a beginning, a new me. I'm tired to death of myself. I can't wait for it to start.' She sank back into her seat as though exhausted by her outburst.

'I, on the other hand,' said Canon Beagle, his eye fixed on the road ahead, 'am looking in my pilgrimage for an end, something final. A consummation almost.'

CHAPTER THREE

He Who Would Valiant Be

'All out,' said the driver without turning round.

There was a flurry of movement behind him as the passengers got themselves together. Mr Guy Tussock and his bicycle got off. Mr and Mrs Clutton Brock and their cello got off. Mrs Lemming and her easel got off. Canon Beagle and his wheelchair were got off. Theodore swung her small leather holdall down from the rack, felt herself rather underaccoutred, and got off.

They appeared to be in the middle of a field. A rutted path bounded by banks of sheep-nibbled thyme wound away into the distance. There was no habitation in sight.

'Where are we?' Mrs Lemming asked. The enquiry, the querulous tone, came naturally to her.

'There's clearly been a mistake,' Clutton Brock turned to the driver. 'Mr, er . . .?'

'Bough,' said the driver. 'Tom Bough.'

'Well, this isn't the entrance, Mr Bough. I remember it quite well. Have we broken down?'

'Nope. House rules. All pilgrims to walk the last two miles.'

'Impossible,' said Mrs Lemming.

'New since my day,' admitted Canon Beagle. 'Bit of a challenge.' But he didn't seem daunted.

Theodora breathed the fresh air, smelt the new hay and remarked the long shadow of the hills in the distance. I've come from one place of learning to another, she thought. Her spirits rose. It was going to be all right.

'We are pilgrims after all,' she said.

'S'right,' the driver agreed. 'Not a holiday. Not yer annual beano at Blackpool.'

It looked as though Clutton Brock might do Bough some violence. Theodora stepped in quickly.

'We'll walk, of course. But could you take some of our luggage?'

Bough looked doubtful. 'Orders are pilgrims carry their own luggage. What you bring, you carry.'

'Come on,' said Canon Beagle, 'Be a sport. They're too old.' He looked with derision at his companions.

'I'm not,' said Clutton Brock. He put a protective arm around the cello.

'How about if we do a deal,' Canon Beagle cajoled. 'You take the luggage, we'll take the extras. That seems to keep the spirit of the rule. Yes?'

'I'll take Mrs – it's Mrs Lemming, isn't it? – your easel if you'll allow me.' Canon Beagle hoisted it on to his lap. 'And you'll push us, yes?' he enquired of Theodora.

'Yes,' said Theodora, 'with pleasure.'

'Just what I need,' said Guy Tussock, bending to reassemble his machine. 'A bit of a spin. I'll go on ahead.' He tried in vain to line up the two wheels of the bicycle. Then looked with his boyish smile at the only able-bodied man. 'Do you think you could possibly hold an end for me?'

Mr Clutton Brock laid the cello on the grass and wedged the front wheel between his knees.

'Thanks awfully,' said Guy, then swung himself on to his machine, did something complicated to the gears and, after a couple of effortful heaves on the peddles, gathered speed up the track.

'Right you are then,' Bough said and without further delay hoisted himself back into the cab. He too did something horrible to the gears and reversed the bus back down the track.

The little party set off.

Canon Beagle sang, 'He who would valiant be 'gainst all disaster,' in a serviceable tenor. Theodora pushed him. Mrs Lemming trotted behind and joined in with a breathy alto. The Clutton Brocks followed a little apart and behind them. Mr Clutton Brock carried the cello and blew his nose a good deal. He seemed to be afflicted with hay fever. The heat was considerable. They sweated, some from exertion, some from unsuitable dress. Behind her, Theodora could hear the irregular panting of Mr Clutton Brock. She glanced back and saw his wife walking at some distance from him. Her long lean face with its abundance of faded fair hair was partly turned away from them gazing towards the woods on their right. She wore a dark blue silk dress. In her hand she carried a mauve parasol held high above her head. It waved about like a flag, it's uncertain shade darting too and fro in front of her. Mrs Lemming was beginning to whimper.

'It's not quite what I'd imagined, what I'd hoped for.'

'That's life,' said Canon Beagle cheerfully.

'Well it's all right for you,' Mrs Lemming retorted with spirit. 'You're being pushed.'

Canon Beagle was priest enough to refrain from remarking that his arthritis did not flourish in the heat and that every jolt of the uneven path pained him.

'Perhaps if you put a hand on the chair,' Theodora said, 'it'll help to balance you.'

Mrs Lemming was not so far gone in self-pity that she could not react to kindness. Gratefully she stretched out a hand. They trundled on.

'It's all part of the training, you know,' Canon Beagle said. 'Bellaire felt that to get the most out of a pilgrimage or a retreat you have to make an effort, empty yourself a bit.'

'Whatever do you mean?' exclaimed Mrs Lemming.

'Well, having to arrive on your own two feet, there being no transport, no telephone, no TV or wireless, no newspapers, no electric light, it's all part of the emptying process.'

'No lights?' Mrs Lemming stopped in her tracks. Theodora thought she might be about to bolt back to Tunbridge Wells.

'It's all right.' Mrs Clutton Brock had come alongside

the wheelchair group. She was tall and given extra height by the parasol. She towered above Mrs Lemming and was almost on an eye-level with Theodora who was six foot one.

Mrs Clutton Brock's voice was low and dramatic. 'You'll find it's quite all right. I was here, oh, years ago when Augustine was just getting underway. No one had much experience of retreat houses for laity in those days. He had to experiment, find out what contributed to the spiritual life, what people would stand. He kept inventing things we weren't allowed to do. But he wasn't silly. He was feeling his way towards a disciplined life, a rhythm of prayer and work, simplicity, silence, space, a way of life which prepares for death.'

'Death,' gasped Mrs Lemming. 'But I'm looking for life. I haven't begun to live yet. My husband . . .' She stopped in confusion.

'The odd thing was,' Canon Beagle said, 'though one half of him wanted just what you've said, a way of life which was stripped and simple, the other part of him was rather theatrical. All that fancy dress he would keep strutting about in. I've never seen chasubles like them. He could have been Lyon King-of-Arms. That cope he wore for St Sylvan's festal Eucharist. I'll swear it had his deer-hounds embroidered on it.'

Theodora was aware of a squat shadow impinging on the group. Mr Clutton Brock held up his hand dramatically. 'Look,' he said, Cortez upon Darien. 'There it is. Here we are.'

Below them in a slight hollow ringed with wooded

hills on three sides was the chapel with the guest-house and the short avenue of chestnut trees linking them. The clock on the chapel tower stood at six o'clock. There was a white flag flying from the roof of the house, too far away to make out its device. The little huddle of buildings looked serene in the late afternoon sun. Far to the left could be glimpsed the pediment of Broadcourt.

'Where's the well?' asked Mrs Lemming. 'The holy well of St Sylvan?'

'Behind the chapel, a little way up into the hills,' Mrs Clutton Brock answered her as though talking to herself.

'Hidden from profane view,' added her husband. So there are three of them who have been before, Theodore thought, Canon Beagle and the Clutton Brocks. She glanced across at Mr Clutton Brock's tweed-clad figure. His shoulders, she noticed were tense, his hands clenched the black cello case. His wife swayed her parasol away from him and began to stride forward down the slope towards the guest-house.

Guy manoeuvred his bicycle between the ruts, negotiated patches of shingle mistakenly scattered to fill potholes and fell into a rhythm. He felt exhilarated to be freed from the company of his fellow travellers. Not that he would allow his behaviour to be constrained by them. Early in life he'd resolved to take all he could and evade those who wished to thwart him. It was not a matter of selfishness but of self-preservation. If he didn't take precautions for himself, no one else would, he felt. He had not known his parents for very long; they had died in a car crash before he was eleven. He had gone to live with his grandparents, Canon and Mrs Tussock, since no one else could think of a better solution for his care. Whilst he was alive his father, a reluctant accountant, had seemed to want him to be and do all sorts of things he didn't want to be or do. Guy had evolved a quiver full of techniques for evading becoming what his father wanted him to be. When his father died Guy simply continued in his grandfather's house in the way he had begun with his father. He'd perfected not being around. He practised and made perfect a way of lying which was difficult to detect or which it was difficult to distinguish from joking or irony. Whether he'd consciously decided to transmute his anxieties into jokiness, he had by now forgotten. It had become his character, his style. He became proficient at getting from people what he needed, which was often no more than an assurance that he was there, that he existed. His demands were not exorbitant: a shared acknowledgement of an opinion or perception, a collusion in a joke often sufficed. Giving him orders, however, telling him what to think, had no effect on him. He took to his bike in an instant and was gone.

Now he was freewheeling down the hill towards what his father had hated and his grandfather had loved. He knew his father's life had been based on his hatred of *his* father's life. Guy had researched the matter. He had needed to orientate himself. He had listened to the conversation of grown-ups and made his inferences. Ben Tussock had expected his son to be a jolly evangelical boy scout. But his only child, born to him late, had taken after his mother. He would laugh at things Ben did not understand. Guy the grandson, in his turn, had got on well with his grandmother in an oblique sort of way before she had retired into her dementia. She understated things which her husband, with his vocabulary of professional enthusiasm, had not noticed or would have taken differently. Our family is based on disappointing our fathers. I am in a noble tradition, he said, to comfort himself. As he pushed his wheels round, he thought, well now in my new circumstances perhaps I can make a new start, here, now, this time. He reached the top of the rise and let his feet drag in the bumpy grass. He braked and gazed down with curiosity at what he had seen only once before. There was a flag flying from the guest-house. He could make out the device. A Roman soldier in black on a white ground, standing between the antlered head of a golden deer. 'My birthright,' he murmured and grinned hugely in the direction of the guest-house.

In the kitchen of the guest-house Ruth Swallow finished shelling the last of the broad beans, leaned back in her chair and yawned. She wore her thick dark hair loosely coiled in heavy plaits which she fixed to her head with pins so that the two ends met on top of her head and stood up like the ears of a startled horse. They gave her the air of one who might have an additional sense. Her face had a heavyness which made her look older than her thirty years. Some men had wanted to draw her, others considered her plain. Some found her formidable, others scarcely noticed her. Behind her on the mantelshelf the large clock clicked towards half-past six.

She took stock of her domain. New bread was proving under a damp cloth on the low stone windowsill; the gas purred under a kettle of water on the stove; three sorts of beans and a vast bowl of lentils occupied the far end of the table. A mound of raspberries gave off a sweet perfume in the warm air. Fruits of the earth and work of human hands, my hands, she thought. She was content. Why couldn't it go on? It met a need, heaven knew. Sometimes, in the evening, we would sit at the table and meditate on the long history of the place. Legend affirmed that this farm had been built on the site of St Sylvan's own house. The bricks in the wall were Roman and the flags beneath her feet those which perhaps he had trod. As he had worked to create a small centre of Christian civilisation at a time when much threatened it, so they, Tom and Angus and the little group of pious men and women who helped here and came regularly to support the pilgrims and retreatants, laboured to create a different world to the one which existed ten miles down the road.

She looked towards the tray laid for six, checked the number of scones and then moved towards the stove. She poured water from the simmering kettle on to an earthenware teapot, assembled milk and mugs and then moved towards the mantelshelf. She took down the rose-wood sewing-box and laid it on the table. From it she extracted a role of silken stuff and spread it out. The stone flags of the kitchen floor were cool to her bare feet.

Her movements were slow, not clumsy but deliberate like those of someone performing a ritual properly, attentively. Ruth aimed at the complete, the integrated life not consciously but out of instinct. She did not see herself as a virtuous peasant, though others, less discerning, were tempted to. She had reigned in her kitchen kingdom for seven years and now she was to be deposed.

The open back door let in a scent of hay and stocks from the garden. Near at hand large earthenware tubs held herbs: basil, rosemary, parsley, lemon mint and dill. They'll not want those, she thought. They won't want that sort of cooking. After a moment or two, when she judged the tea would have brewed, she went to the door, put her hand against the jamb to support the weight growing within and called, 'Tom.'

His considerable figure came round the corner, wiping his hands free of diesel.

'Did you leave them at the causeway?'

He nodded. 'It'll take them half an hour. They're not wick, except for the girl. One of em's in a wheelchair.'

'It's hot for walking.'

'It's hot for driving.' He took the teapot from her hand and poured steadily into the two mugs.

'Angus here yet?'

She nodded 'He's saying evensong in the chapel. He'll be back in time to meet them. He's very reliable.'

'There's been no bother from the Sunday party, special requirements like?' He raised his head from his tea. Sweat gathered on his brow from the hot liquid.

'Not a word, love. Don't get so het up.'

46

'I can't think why they have to come here at all. They could make their choice anywhere. I wonder they have the nerve to look us in the face.'

'Oh, Tom, it's not their fault. They think it's the money.'

'They're bad managers. They know nothing about money.'

'You've only heard that, Tom. We probably couldn't do any better. Anyway perhaps there's going to be money,' said Ruth, more to placate Tom than to tell a truth she actually believed. 'We don't know for certain there isn't.' Her wish to calm him, to mother him, betrayed itself in her tone. She hated emotions to be random or greater than the situation warranted. They should have their proper object. A wild lashing of anger or fear always called up her pity. She put her arms lightly over Tom's shoulders. He was, she saw, soothed. He did not shake her off. She was stronger than he. He might resort to violence to cope. She would help to keep him from that.

'Nor for certain that there is.'

'Tussock never loved this place like Father Augustine did.'

'No but he knew its uses,' said Tom. 'It had its uses didn't it, love?'

'Who's this Tussock that's coming with this party?' Ruth asked to steer him away from his dangerous ground. 'Is he related?'

'I don't know. He's about the right age. Looks about twelve and a half but he may be a bit older. Nice bike.'

Ruth half-turned in her chair. Guy's long shadow belied his short figure. Carefully he edged round the door and shyly intruded the handlebars of his machine. Tom didn't acknowledge his presence.

'Can I bring my bike in?' Guy asked.

'Why?' Bough asked.

'I like to keep it close. It's all I've got.' Guy glanced experimentally at Tom and then at Ruth.

'Are you of the party?' Ruth enquired.

'I'm bound for Heaven. Yes.' Guy wasn't an Open University student for nothing. 'I'm Guy Tussock,' he said.

'We were just wondering', Ruth said, 'whether you were any relation. Canon Tussock . . .'

'Was my grandad.' Guy sounded as though this was a line he'd had to speak before.

Ruth smiled and put out her hand. 'You're very welcome, Guy. Of course you can bring your bicycle in. It'll go between the fridge and the dresser quite nicely.'

For a moment Guy feared she was going to embrace him and backed away. But the danger, if it were one, passed.

'You haven't been to us before then?' Tom seemed disposed to be friendly.

'Not lately actually, not visited as such,' Guy answered.

'Your grandad, of course, used to bring his groups regularly.'

Guy nodded.

'Would you like to see your room? When the others come there'll be a cup in the library and Mr Bootle'll give his introduction to the place.'

Guy had many ways of dealing with people who tried to organise him. Sometimes he feigned deafness or imbecility. Sometimes he agreed with what they said whilst continuing to pursue his own path. It was a measure of his liking for Ruth that he bothered to share his plans.

'I thought I'd camp,' he said. 'Up by the well. Yes?'

Ruth looked at Bough. 'One less with the sheets,' he said.

'I suppose I ought to ask Mr Bootle. You'll want your food here though, won't you?' Ruth didn't care to be rejected at so fundamental a level.

'Rather,' Guy used his smile. 'Bread smells good.'

'It can't matter now the place is falling apart,' Bough said.

'Trade slack?' Guy enquired.

'There'd be nothing wrong with trade if they'd only make up their minds to support the place instead of shilly-shallying,' Ruth answered him.

'Who's they?'

'The diocese,' said Bough. 'The powers that be. They don't want places like this. We don't fit in. We are very different from the norm.' He sounded as though he might be quoting someone.

'Oh it's not that, Tom,' Ruth calmed him. 'It's money. And, of course, we don't make money and Bishop Peake's never liked us. He couldn't stand Father Augustine.'

'So what with the accountants and the squabbling between churchmanships and the Church not knowing what it should be doing for the world, it looks as though we're sunk.' Bough would not be diverted from his line.

'What do they want to do with you?'

'A heritage centre,' said Bough with relish. 'Tudor feasts. Blokes in tights and women spinning. And other people watching them.' His tone suggested delight at the sheer idiocy of the thing.

'About as daft as you could get,' Ruth agreed.

'What'll happen to you?'

'They haven't thought of that yet,' Ruth answered.

'Or ever,' Tom said.

'Won't they need you?'

'I'm not dressing up in funny clothes.' He rubbed the back of his stubble neck. Guy attempted to visualise him as a tudor peasant.

'We've got a job,' Ruth said. 'A proper job. People need places like this to be real in, not bits of silly make-believe to escape from being real in.'

'Grandad used to say refreshment was important not diversion,' Guy said.

'He got that from Father Augustine,' said Ruth.

'Like much of his thinking,' said Guy with sudden acuteness.

'Did you know your grandad well?' Ruth asked.

'My mum and dad died when I was eleven so I went to live with Grandfather Ben and Grandma. I've only just left home,' Guy said with pride. 'Did you know him?' he asked Ruth.

Ruth nodded. 'A bit. I came here seven years ago. It was about this time of year. Canon Tussock brought one last party here before he retired. I think it was a sort of reunion of his people who'd come in earlier times.' She turned to Tom. 'Tom's always been here, on and off, so you knew him quite well, didn't you, Tom?'

'I've always been here and my dad too. My dad knew your grandad.' He eyed Guy. 'He's still alive. You'll have to . . .' He broke off. There was the sound of voices loud and demanding in the hall. The pilgrims had arrived.

'I think I'll just slip out and pitch my tent,' said Guy, and did.

CHAPTER FOUR

'Gainst All Disaster

'Pilgrimage', said the Reverend Angus Bootle in his precise Edinburgh accent, 'is always to one end. And that end is death.'

Theodora recognised familiar ground and allowed her attention to wander round the library in which the pilgrims were gathered. Bodily needs had been assuaged, the rigours of the journey to some extent repaired. The remains of Ruth's scones adhered to Canon Beagle's waistcoat as he sat in his wheelchair to Theodora's left. Mrs Lemming clasped a half-drunk cup of Indian tea; the Clutton Brocks sipped camomile. Guy, who had arrived late, perched, poised for flight, on the end of the sofa occupied by Theodora and toyed with a glass of springwater. The library in the modern part of the guest-house, large, airy with few books, gave on to the garden. Through the open french windows came the sound of a tractor in the distance.

Mrs Lemming leaned forward with clamorous attention, her eyes riveted on Angus as though he might hold the secret of life.

'And there are two sorts of death, death of the body and death of the ego,' Angus was continuing.

Theodora brought her attention back to him. His brown hair was sleek but his beard was curly. She wondered why she felt this combination to be particularly Victorian. And if he had a curly beard, surely he ought to have curly hair to match. Did it represent a divided nature? In other respects he could not have been more modern. He wore fawn trousers and a green shirt surmounted by a clerical collar. His feet were clad in sandles and socks. He could have been an old thirty-five or a young fifty. His demeanour was of one who exercised great control over himself as though he feared any display of energy or indeed originality of thought might frighten his pilgrims and deter them from their search. He stood at a table referring occasionally to small sheets of writing paper. Mostly, however, he fixed his attention on each pilgrim in turn.

'Death of the body is, of course,' his voice smiled in deprecation, 'inevitable. But death of the ego is not. The true pilgrim seeks to reduce his destructive ego and so save his soul. I use the generic masculine', he said carefully, 'to include the female sex.'

A sound suspiciously like a snore emanated from the direction of Canon Beagle's wheelchair. Theodora wondered whether she should wake him up. What was the state of his destructive ego? She was saved from the need to act by Mr Clutton Brock clearing his throat and saying loudly, 'I came here to pray. I need to pray regularly. I need help. I feel,' he looked round accusingly as though this might be someone's fault, 'I feel lost.'

Angus paused and gave him the measure of his careful attention. 'Aye,' he said, 'Aye, that's very good. That's a good place from which to start a spiritual journey.' The Scottish accent was prominent. 'Perhaps if I run through the domestic arrangements you will see that they have been evolved by our founder, the Reverend Augustine Bellaire, who was perhaps known to some of you, to meet just those needs which', he consulted one of his bits of paper, 'Mr Clutton Brock has mentioned.'

He shuffled his papers and extracted the appropriate one.

'Prayers are said in the chapel at eight o'clock in the morning, five-thirty in the afternoon and nine o'clock in the evening. The eight o'clock service is a Eucharist, the five-thirty an evensong and the nine o'clock compline. The chapel is open throughout the day for private prayer and meditation. The sacrament is reserved.'

Mrs Lemming thought how much Norman would have disapproved. It must have changed since his day, since Tussock's retirement.

Angus had switched from soul to body. 'Breakfast is at eight-forty-five, lunch at one and supper at seven-thirty. A cup of tea', he smiled at the trolley in their midst, 'is served here at four-thirty. The evening meal is taken in silence and silence is kept until breakfast the following morning. With regard to the rhythm of the week, it is usual for us to conclude our time together with a procession to the well of St Sylvan and to celebrate a Eucharist there on the last morning.' Angus cleared his throat and girded his loins. 'This year there are several reasons for this being a very special occasion. It is by tradition the feast day of St Sylvan as well as being by legend the day of his martyrdom. Our neighbours from nearby parishes, some church groups, a number of people of traveller descent, generally come along. It is, moreover, an important juncture in the life of this foundation.' Angus's noble brow puckered for an instant and then he resumed. 'You will, therefore, on your last day with us, have an opportunity to join in our celebrations.'

'What happens the rest of the time?' It was Guy's voice. Mrs Lemming turned to look at him. 'I'd thought I might get to know some of the countryside. I've got a bike, you see,' he said as though letting Angus into a secret. 'And I've got a lot to do.'

Theodora wondered what that might be. She had seen little of Guy at the Open University week. He had not, after all, been in her group but she'd heard one of her colleagues say Tussock never wasted a minute.

'I haven't got very much to do,' Mrs Lemming said. 'But I thought I might try a little sketching.' She looked round as though someone might object to so extravagant an activity.

'We've brought our cello,' said Mr Clutton Brock, wiping his watering eyes and entering into the competition.

'Father Augustine's rule was that pilgrims should, within the framework of communal prayer, find their own rhythm of work, rest and reading. This may well be different for each of you. Certainly exploring the countryside, sketching, music-making or, if you should feel so inclined, gardening are all perfectly acceptable activities. If we each do all that we choose to do with complete attention to that thing we shall find ourselves new made over. I shall be available to any who would like advice about reading or the disposition of time while you are with us. As you may have heard, we have no newspapers, wireless, television or telephone. It was Father Augustine's intention that as pilgrims we should withdraw from the trivial anxieties of the world and seek to reunite ourselves with what is of infinite value, wheresoever each of us may find that thing.'

'What about electricity?' It was Mrs Lemming's voice.

Angus smiled his reassuring smile. 'Father Augustine himself found it helpful to be without electric light during the hours of darkness. He felt the essential nature of the Christian symbolism of light shining in darkness could only properly be understood if darkness was a daily and inescapable experience. But that doesn't mean that there's no electricity here. The gentlemen will find electric shavers in their rooms and there are fridges and hoovers in the domestic apartments. The showers will be hot in the mornings. Though not always', he admitted, 'in the evenings.'

Theodora wondered how consistent this was. If darkness was an essential spiritual experience, why not cold or raw or rotting food? However, she was game for anything.

'We all want something', said Canon Beagle suddenly

jerking out of sleep. 'We've all come to get something. Tusk used to say that.' He fixed his eye on Angus. 'You're too young to remember Canon Tussock, I dare say.'

'I had the pleasure of meeting the Canon on a number of occasions. The last was at his reunion party seven years ago when he retired. Moreover, if I may say so,' – he consulted his list – 'Canon Beagle, what we want and what we get may not be the same thing. Our wanting something does not constitute a good reason for having it. We are in the Lord's hands. The form of our death, both natural and spiritual, will not be apparent until the end.'

All good apocalyptic stuff, Theodora thought. Nor does Angus scruple to teach his grandmother to suck eggs. She would not herself have ventured to address Canon Beagle in such tones. Canon Beagle had the tips of his fingers pressed together but didn't seem to resent Angus's remarks. Perhaps he recognised a fellow professional.

Angus shuffled his papers and cleared his throat. 'I think that is more than enough from me at the moment. It remains for me to wish you all a pleasant and profitable sojourn with us. I hope you will not allow any of our present difficulties to cloud your concentration on whatever it is that has brought you to us. I think you will find the domestic arrangements comfortable. If there is anything you want, our excellent housekeeper, Mrs Swallow, Ruth, will be happy to help you. She is assisted in her duties by Mr Tom Bough whom I think you have already met. There is access for the disabled to all ground-floor rooms,' – he glanced kindly at Canon

Beagle who looked disappointed – 'and of course to the chapel. As some of you will know, I am the incumbent of the parish church of St Sylvan and All Angels in the village of St Sylvan at Rest. For the period of the retreat, however, I shall be sleeping in the guest-house in room twelve. Oh, and if any of you should wish to telephone your relations, perhaps to assure them of your safe arrival, you will find the public phone box very conveniently situated in the village at the end of the lane a little to the left of the signpost. It is a most pleasant walk of about two and a half miles. Shall we end with the grace?'

The little group eased itself from the embrace of the armchairs and dutifully applied to the Holy Trinity for grace, love and fellowship.

The portrait of Father Augustine Bellaire, the founder, dominated the entrance hall. Theodora, longing for fresh air and solitude after the stuffy drive, found she could not pass it by without contemplating it. It hung on the wall opposite the front door and a shaft of evening light slashed it from top to bottom, illuminating the face. Father Bellaire had been painted in the scarlet-and-white robe of the Warden of the Shrine of St Sylvan, designed by himself on the lines of a Knight of the Garter. He exhibited considerable physical presence. Theodora scrutinised the face. It was that of a man in late middle age with a good growth of silvery fair hair worn rather long and curling round the ears. The face was emaciated and ascetic, the eyes pale and far apart, slanting upwards like a deer's. The lips of the wide mouth were thin and to them the painter had imparted an air of sensitivity, which, however, as Theodora looked upon them, seemed to lack charity. In his right hand Father Augustine clasped a book; his left rested on a biretta placed next to a crucifix on a table beside him. The overall effect was of an Edwardian Shakespearian actor. Turning from the portrait Theodora saw the same biretta preserved in a glass case on the table in the middle of the hall. He had liked tranklements then, Father Augustine?

What had he been like in real life, she wondered, besides being handsome and pious? She wished she'd met him. And what about Benjamin Tussock? There was no portrait of him to be seen. What had these two, by all accounts, very disparate personalities had in common that they should both have come together to organise retreats for Anglican pilgrims? Had there been conflict? Surely there must have been tension. Both were opinionated and their views were located at different ends of the spectrum of churchmanship.

She turned away from the detritus of a life, the influence of which she felt pervaded the whole atmosphere of the place and pushed on into the open air. She recalled Canon Beagle's remark, 'We have all come here for something.' What had she come for? If she was honest she supposed she'd come to get away from Geoffrey's marriage preparations. She'd worked as a curate at Betterhouse for just over a year and had thought she knew and appreciated her vicar, Geoffrey Brighouse, quite well enough to be confident of his common sense in all important matters. She'd reckoned without the irrational impulses, both Geoffrey's and indeed her own. Geoffrey had briefly met and instantly proposed to a colleague of his sister's, Oenone Troutbeck. Oenone taught English at a smart independent girls' school. She had a commanding presence and a sound opinion of her own worth. Theodora had been amazed and then, to her shame, jealous. She had grown more and more irritated with Geoffrey as she watched him apply his energy and intelligence, usually given without stint to the parish's affairs, to the trivia of marriage preparation. She did not in the least want to marry Geoffrey herself, so the debilitating and unfamiliar emotion took her by surprise and left her tired and out of temper both with herself and with Geoffrey. A retreat, a space to confront and discipline her disorderly emotions was what she told herself she needed. She had seven days to take herself in hand. The easy and wrong thing to do would be to plan; instead she'd leave herself open to events. Let the spirit flow, she told herself, and trust in it.

She had arrived in her peregrination at the back door of the kitchen. It stood open, guarded by large pots of herbs. Rosemary and marjoram scented the early evening air. Theodora hesitated. The door was open. It invited. She stepped inside. The preparations for the evening meal were evident. All was tidy. Plates were stacked to warm on the aga. Pans simmered quietly as though pursuing a life of their own. On the table a wooden sewing-box stood open to disclose its organised contents of threads and needles, thimbles and scissors, as esoteric to

Theodora as a surgeon's trolley. The feeling that this was someone else's domain impinged. It would be an intrusion to stay. Theodora turned and made her way out into the garden. Just turning in through the wicket gate at the far end were Ruth and Tom, hand in hand. They looked, Theodora thought, partnered, joined man and wife. She thought of Geoffrey and instantly regretted doing so.

'They're terribly good,' said a voice at her elbow. 'Just ripe and flavoursome.'

Theodora glanced down and detected at knee-level the small form of Guy Tussock crouched between a row of raspberry canes. He extended his hand and offered her the fruit.

'The grub's going to be OK,' his tone suggested she had voiced some fear to the contrary. 'They grow a lot of their own.' He indicated the rows of onions and beans, potatoes and leeks, as orderly it its way as the kitchen. 'This is my kingdom,' Guy observed. He gestured round the garden and pointed to the huge mulberry tree in the centre which divided the flower garden from the vege-table. 'Cosmic trees, the lot. The whole works.'

I'm the king of the castle, Theodora thought. She liked the idea of Guy claiming the place as his kingdom. Would this point to his being a relation of Ben Tussock? 'So we're all set to learn,' she said recalling her last conversation with Guy.

'Could be,' he extended his arm round the whole of the pleasant space. 'Grandad always said they were good providers.'

'You're a relation then of Canon Tussock?' Theodora was tentative. She felt it was intrusive to ask a direct question about someone's relations but she was genuinely curious. She liked to get such matters straight.

Guy parted the raspberry canes and stood up. A stray tendril had entwined itself in his hair. He looked like some sprite of the place, either more or less than human. His eyes as he smiled up at her were small and unblinking. 'Yes. Tusk was my grandad.' His grin widened. 'I'm the new young master. I'm the successor to Father Bellaire.'

Angus Bootle said grace and there was a scraping of chairs as the pilgrims took their places for their first supper. The silence that followed was precarious. People drew breath to converse and then remembered and desisted. The sound of knifes wrestling with pork cutlet or nut roast, as the individual regimen dictated, was unnaturally loud. The splash of water in glass resounded like a bath filling. Deprived of the cover of conversation, eye contact was embarrassing and therefore avoided. We do not know how to cope, Theodora thought as she addressed her chop. It is as though we are being punished. We shall have to work at this to turn it into something positive. She had made a silent retreat before her own deaconing but that occasion had been completely silent apart from the celebration of the liturgy. Then, too, she had been with people going through the same training as herself. She could recall no strain then, only peace. She tried to recollect how she had behaved. Where ought we to put our thoughts? On our food? But though this was delicious it seemed too carnal to take all one's attention. Should she simply notice her own thoughts? But at present she had none and when she had any they tended to take the form of thinking about Geoffrey and that was distressing. She would concentrate on the silence itself then.

They were all seated at one long table in a dining-room the same size as the library but without the scattering of books which that room had. Here there was nothing to take the eye. There was no furniture apart from the table and chairs. White walls enclosed them on three sides and on the fourth the open window gave a view to the *hortus conclusus* beyond. The only decoration, though that was no name by which to call it, was a large black wooden cross fixed to the wall above Angus's head.

Mr and Mrs Clutton Brock sat opposite her. Canon Beagle was on her left. Mrs Clutton Brock was sipping water with a gesture which suggested it might have been claret, her eyes fixed on the ceiling. Mr Clutton Brock was dealing with some soya confection as though this required his whole attention. Canon Beagle was having difficulty with his teeth.

To her left Guy had his head down, eating with the ravenous concentration of the still-growing young and working his way through a mound of the excellent spinach, to which every now and then he applied lavish quantities of butter from the dish which he seemed to have commandeered. Angus ate as though he were performing a duty, punctiliously but without apparent enjoyment.

At that point she became aware of a restlessness beside her. Mrs Lemming was clearing her throat and shuffling her elbows in a meaningful way. Theodora inferred the need for salt. Of course, that was what was required, a calm attentiveness to the needs of others. She edged the salt in the direction of Mrs Lemming and glanced round to see if other of her neighbours was in want. They were all coping.

The silence grew more familiar. They began to be more comfortable with it. It was an event when Mrs Clutton Brock managed with a single elegant eyebrow to summon the bread from Canon Beagle's end of the table without, as it were, interrupting the flow of things. Smiling was allowed. Theodora turned and smiled at Mrs Lemming who, after a moment's hesitation, returned it.

The cat when it appeared at the open window felt like a temptation. He paused for a moment on the sill and then plopped heavily down into the room and progressed silently across the bare floorboards. He was large and muscular with long black hair. His eye had that remote concentrated look of the hunter and from his mouth hung the limp furry form of his latest prey. Guy paused in mid-mouthful and went white. The silence turned expectant. All except Angus ceased to eat and fixed their eyes on the animal. The cat continued his deliberate progress round the edge of the room and stopped opposite the door. Mrs Clutton Brock rose and opened it for him. Without sparing her a look, he stalked out still holding his burden. The pilgrims settled back again bound together as though by some common victory.

Their silence could deal, they felt, with whatever should be thrown at them.

The final hurdle came into view. Theodora recognised it as a familiar one. It was a question of timing. Four years at an English girls' boarding school and another four at an Oxford college had left her with an eating rate well above the socially accepted norm. She tried slowing down. Gazing at an empty plate for ten minutes while Canon Beagle got command over his teeth and caught up would be more than trying. In the event they finished more or less together. Plates were passed up and Angus doled out the queen's pudding with mathematical precision. The concluding grace sounded and they scraped their chairs again, the first challenge of their common life triumphantly accomplished.

Theodora had crossed the hall and reached the top of the staircase when she heard the scream. There was a sound of thudding footsteps as she turned back. In the fading light, which inside the house was darker than outside the windows, she discerned Mrs Lemming standing in the middle of the hall in front of the glass case which held Father Bellaire's biretta. Theodora's instinct was to reach for the electric-light switch but the click produced no answering illumination. The electricity had, of course, been turned off, presumably at the mains, to insure the keeping of the night hours according to Father Bellaire's rule. Mrs Lemming clutched her arm and pointed to the case. Under the biretta could just be seen the yellowish-white shape of a human skull.

The phone box beamed its rays into the surrounding

darkness like a lighthouse. It was the old-fashioned kind
made of bomb-proof glass panes encased in a solid red
painted metal fame. It appeared and disappeared from
view as Theodora strode along the winding lane from St
Sylvan's towards the village. The scene in the hall of an
hour ago kept replaying itself in her imagination.

Mrs Lemming's cries had summoned the rest of the
pilgrims. At first it was not clear what had caused her
emotion. Guy had been early on the scene. He raised
the glass case and whipped off the biretta. Then as
though elevating the paten he'd raised the skull and held
it on high. Mr Clutton Brock marched up, gazed at the
object and then turned on his heel and swung off across
the hall and out through the front door. Mrs Clutton
Brock, who was much taller than Guy, stared down at
the skull and then ran her finger over the cranium. She
looked at the dust which came off and adhered to her
finger. As she did so, Theodora noticed that in the middle
of the skull above the hole, where, in life, the nose would
be, was a glint of metal. She looked more closely and
detected a nail with a broad head which had been
inserted cleanly into the bone. Angus, meanwhile, busied
himself with examining the glass case which had housed
the object. Canon Beagle, who had bowled up later
than the rest, looked at it, sucked the air through his
teeth and muttered, 'How very foolish.' The group must,
Theodora thought, have presented to any observer an
ikon of different responses to mortality.

Mrs Lemming was not easily calmed and the Reverend
Angus Bootle's unwillingness to break the rule of silence
did not make it any easier. Theodora could see that he

felt that the rule had been made to help pilgrims to cope on just such occasions as this. However much Mrs Lemming wanted to give full vent to nervous hysteria it was impossible, in the face of Angus's calm determination, not to practise self-control. Gently Angus took the skull from Guy's hands. He gathered up the biretta and replaced the glass case, now empty, on the table. Then he signalled to Theodora to see Mrs Lemming to her room. He smiled reassuringly at Mrs Lemming as though this were normal procedure in any well-run retreat house.

Theodora had accompanied the shaking woman up the staircase to the first floor. Her room was exactly like Theodora's own, a small white cell, absolutely without decoration, comprising of a door, a window, a bed, a table and a chair, and a notice in Gothic script giving instructions about what to do in case of fire. Your cell shall teach you all you need to know, Theodora thought. Mrs Lemming's only impact on the place was an open suitcase and a mass of coat hangers on the table. The light, by this time almost gone, prevented any consoling pastime like reading. Touched by a sudden inspiration, Theodora mimed the action of drinking. She had in mind a cup of hot milk. Mrs Lemming, however, dived into the jumble of her suitcase, scrabbled in its innards for a moment, threw out a couple of balls of stockings and in triumph produced a large Edwardian racegoer's leather-and-silver flask. Theodora declined the offer of a swig and felt able to leave the lady to her consolation.

Now, as she swung along the track towards the light,

she rather wished she'd taken the proferred hospitality. She realised how very tired she was. The image of the skull kept dancing before her eyes. Who had placed it beneath the biretta and why? Was it a joke or a threat? A mockery of Father Augustine's style or a reminder of mortality for the present pilgrims? She was nearly sure it had not been in place when she went into supper. She tried to recall the order in which they had appeared in the dining-room. She and Angus had gone in together, Guy had been soon after, then the Clutton Brocks. That meant Canon Beagle had been last. It was impossible to imagine his doing anything as tasteless or as macabre as placing a biretta on a skull.

She put the problem away from her and pushed on towards the village. Two and a half miles, Angus had said. Surely that must be nearly completed by now. She badly wanted to ring Geoffrey. He wouldn't, she had to admit, be in the least worried about whether she had arrived safely. It never occurred to him that she would not. In any case, he had presumably much to think about. It was, as she acknowledged, sheer self-indulgence. She wanted to hear his sane voice and exchange a few words, it did not matter about what, he would understand her and she him. There was rarely any need to elaborate or explain. The ban on talking, the impossibility of reading without electric light, the abstention from conversation at supper were subjects she'd like to know his mind on. Had he made a silent retreat? she wondered. Surely he must have done before he was priested. There was a great deal she reflected that she did not know about

Geoffrey. Did Oenone know any more? She realised where she was heading and put a stopper on her thoughts.

She was aware of vigorous country nightlife all around her. An owl called at regular intervals; pheasants coughed in the middle distance and down in the village a dog uttered a staccato volley of barks. Every now and again rabbits caught unaware froze or scudded across her path. Sheep could be heard chewing and shuffling about on the other side of the dry-stone walls. The track which had started in open country had got deeper and now narrowed into a passage with high banks on either hand. She rounded the bend and saw the road, the signpost and the phone booth a hundred yards away. She was about to start forward again when she remarked the booth was not empty. She could just make out the familiar figure of Mr Clutton Brock, his face illuminated by the single electric bulb, in animated conversation. Theodora hesitated for a moment and then she swung off down the road towards the village. The main street had a terrace of stone-built cottages from which came the suddenly shocking sound of music from the television sets. She passed on to find a shuttered shop-cum-post office, a couple more houses and at the far end a single light illuminating a sign The Broad Arms. There were no cars parked outside the pub but propped against the wall beside the door was a familiar yellow mountain bike. Beyond and behind the pub she could glimpse the church, presumably Angus's. That appeared to be it as far as the village was concerned.

The phone booth when she reached it again was empty. Theodora clicked the familiar combination of numbers and raised the handset. There was no more than a couple of rings and she heard the familiar voice saying, 'Geoffrey Brighouse here.' Theodora drew breath and then stopped. She held the handset for a moment and heard the name repeated. Then quickly she put the phone back on the cradle. What, after all, was the rule of silence for, if it did not save her from the consolation of idle chatter?

CHAPTER FIVE

Mysterious Way

The pool, a perfect circle, lay in its cradle of rock with a low cliff at its back. The south side was open to the path which wound up from the chapel through a fringe of yew and holly trees. The immediate surrounds of the pool had been tidied up since Augustine Bellaire first tumbled into the landslip which had made St Sylvan's well accessible to pilgrims. The paving flags had been levelled to make a broad terrace all round it. The ilex at which he had vainly clutched in his descent had flourished, grown taller and now overshadowed a quarter of the pool. The carved marble slab with its deer's head and advice (was it Roman, was it Christian?) had been fixed at eye-level to the face of the cliff.

Guy, perched in his tent on the cliff above the well, pulled at the piece of Velcro which secured the flap and snuffed the air. It tasted fresh and watery in the early light. His grandfather was dead. He had got to St Sylvan's and he would make it his own. He was suffused with health and hope. The tent, of orange nylon, big enough to contain only a single sleeping bag, was pitched in a shallow dip between two large, smooth rocks. There were ferns at its door. Guy stared into the slate-grey water of the well immediately below. The still surface invited him. The chapel clock chimed five. He caught up his towel and slipped like a serpent down between the rocks to the water.

Mrs Lemming peered over the bannisters of the guest-house and gazed at the glass case where last night (had she dreamed it?) she'd seen the skull beneath the biretta. This morning there was nothing in the case. Well, better nothing than horror. She took firm hold of her small easel and satchel and tripped downstairs. The front door presented a problem. It had a plethora of locks and bolts. But Mrs Lemming was resolute. She surveyed the devices and came to the conclusion that only one lock was operational. Beside the door was a key on a chain. Which of the three keyholes would it fit? was the question. She fumbled, selected the smallest and applied it. The door swung open. Gleefully she fled down the path in the direction of the well. She had to see the well. She had to possess it. She felt an almost physical thirst for the place. Surely it would heal her, make her a new and more courageous person. She wanted to be purged of a lifetime of Tubridge Wellsishness, of doing what Norman told her, of thinking what Norman wished her to think. Am I worth nothing? she asked herself as she hastened by the chapel and hurried through the trees towards the pool.

The stony path began to climb. Boulders with a fuzz of moss and lichen rose on either hand. She paused to stroke the growth on one of them. Hart's-tongues and *regalis* ferns joined the vegetation. There was a smell of water. She felt her spirits rise. Then she stopped. The track divided. Which way should she go? One path was wider and concreted, the other narrower and looked harder. Why were there no signposts? Why had she been left comfortless? Mrs Lemming consulted her biblical knowledge and chose the narrow path. Then she halted again. On the still air came a sound. It was so strange, so unlooked for that, for a moment, she could not identify it. The soft notes of a cello came through the curtain of trees and rocks. The playing was accomplished, the phrasing of the Elgar secure and commanding; no fumbling amateur was responsible for it. Mrs Lemming rounded the last of the boulders and came out into the open. In the middle of the space she saw the well. Behind it the ground rose in a sheltering cliff. On the left-hand side of the cliff about halfway down, seated on a stone bench, the instrument held against her as though in an embrace was Mrs Clutton Brock. She was dressed in something flowing and purple. Her hair fell forward as she bent to listen to herself. Her eye had the inward look of the totally concentrated. Life, thought Mrs Lemming, and art, that's what I need, not religion. She set down her easel and unpacked her charcoals.

Canon Beagle in his guest-room meditated on his immobility. He'd woken before six and taken a moment to remember where he was. When he'd worked out from observing the cracks on the ceiling that he wasn't in the Bishop Herbert Nursing Home, his spirits had risen. He'd made it, alone, without a care, to his old haunt. Now all he had to do was to pray and enjoy the beauty of the place and the society which had been provided. Angus looked as though he might manage a theological discussion, the Braithwaite girl seemed sensible. Then underlying it all, was his quest: the satisfaction of his wish to know how things had come about between Augustine and Tussock. If enlightenment were offered on that score, his cup would be running over. He could die happy.

He felt so light-hearted that he considered leaving off some of his medication. It taxed him beyond endurance, bits of this, bits of that. But he thought better of it. Didn't want to seize up in a strange place, causing a lot of trouble for people. He knew from experience that, however steady the will, that barrier against pain was necessary to him. He leaned out from his bed and grasped his stick. He had left his window open overnight. He'd thought of all the times he'd lain out under stars in England, South America, China. He'd not lie out again but at least he could open a window without double glazing. It was some small contact with reality. He'd noticed an increasing number of occasions at Bishop Herbert where they curtailed freedoms he could still enjoy or kept him from realities to which he could still respond. It wasn't going to be like that here.

A couple of blackbirds were practising like a choir, going over and over bits to perfect them. A ring-dove

on the chimney pot was talking to himself in that quiet
intimate way they have. He was about to swing himself
from bed to chair when he heard voices. He recognised
them at once, not at first the words but the tones. They
were the tones of people long practised in quarrelling
with each other. As smooth and predictable as opera
recitative and arias he heard the taunt and the response,
the accusation and counter-accusation that stemmed
from the wish to hurt and humiliate which came from
long-stored rancour, pain and desperation. He tried to
shut his ears but the voices were gaining in strength.
Then suddenly they stopped. Agitatedly, in anger, for
what right had human beings to gash and deface each
other in such a way, he hooked his stick towards the
casement and shut it. At the same time he heard the
window of the room above slammed to.

Eager now to be gone from the room and abroad in
the world, Canon Beagle swung the handle of his wheelchair to bring it alongside his bed. Access for the disabled, eh? Well he'd see about that. He'd fight the good
fight to the end. He wouldn't have a helper, a carer, he
framed the word with contempt. He could still dress and
shave himself. Life in the old dog yet. The great thing
was to use every faculty he still possessed. Pity his teeth
had given out. His tongue explored his last remaining
pair. They felt like decaying castles. But his arms, he
clenched his fist and regarded it, were still immensely
strong. The room had been fitted out for the disabled. It
had stout handrails round all four sides and the door
handles were at a height to be reached from the

wheelchair. There was a bar above the bed for heaving on. He heaved himself into his chair and applied himself competently to the wheel to allow himself to shave and dress. His room on the ground floor gave on to a corridor at the end of which was an outside door leading to the garden. Ramps everywhere. Nothing of a challenge.

By the time he'd reached the end of the path to the chapel, however, the going was rougher, uphill and stony. He increased his efforts and his pace. He began to sweat and felt glad of it. Canon Beagle had retained a notion of being fit long after most of his contemporaries had settled for not being. He marked the beginning of the area round the well and remembered how the path narrowed. Perhaps that would defeat him this time. But no, the way divided and the left-hand curve, he perceived, had been widened and concreted for just such as he. Pity really. He paused to regroup.

He was about to resume his efforts, when round the corner between the rocks there came a stout figure. It was dressed in a singlet, crumpled khaki shorts and old-fashioned running shoes. It was sweating profusely. Mr Clutton Brock was jogging, his elbows rigidly bent, his thin fair hair waving in his own breeze. He laboured on, passing within twenty yards and disappeared up behind the pool. He looked at last gasp. Canon Beagle gazed at him with all the compassion of an athlete for the seriously unfit. No word passed between them. Slowly he started heaving at his wheel.

Theodora, striding out ten minutes behind Canon Beagle and eager to savour the morning and bathe herself in the silence and solitude of the well, was brought up short when she edged her way round the final bank of boulders to emerge on to the terrace. On a bench to her left was Mrs Clutton Brock balancing her cello as she rested from her playing. To her right, Mrs Lemming was wielding charcoal on sugar paper, while opposite her she could make out Canon Beagle, his head thrown back as he contemplated from his parked wheelchair the deer's head and inscription. All were studiously avoiding looking at the centre of the pool where, like a young sprite, Guy could be seen throwing water over his naked body.

At breakfast pilgrims could, of course, converse. Freed from the constraints and embarrassments of silence, fresh from the morning Eucharist in the chapel, minds and souls thus catered for, they felt justified in applying themselves to the gratification of bodily needs. Muesli abounded but so too did warm bread, raspberries and an Edwardian collection of scrambled eggs, kippers and mushrooms.

Theodora was interested to notice that no one spoke of their earlier meeting at the well; there was a feeling of complicity as though to hide their experience from Angus. Mrs Clutton Brock had the air of a lifetime's cultivation of sang-froid; Mrs Lemming had two sons of her own; Canon Beagle had spent a good part of his youth in the shower rooms of the very best rugby clubs of three continents. But they were resolved, clearly, to make no mention of the episode. In time Guy had waded to the bank, flicked his towel over his shoulder and hopped spryly into the surrounding ferns.

About seven-forty-five, one by one they had folded easels, corralled cellos into cases, revved up wheelchairs and made for the chapel. Angus had invited Theodora to serve for him and she had done so in the small white, light-filled space. Angus had not preached (he had told them), but he stood at the chancel steps and gave them a thought for the day.

'We have come here,' he had said, 'with luggage. Physically,' he glanced at Canon Beagle, 'we lug our bodies about with us. But we come here too with a backlog of feelings and judgements. Our past life is our impedimenta. Should we perhaps start our time together by considering what we could fruitfully leave beside the road as we start our pilgrimage? We are, after all, moving towards death where we need nothing.'

Theodora glanced at him now as he ladled scrambled egg on to his plate and took a minute amount of mushrooms. She wanted to ask him about the skull under the biretta. Whose was it? Who had placed it there and when and why? And where was the skull now! But in the calm morning light the event seemed unreal and the enquiry out of place. Certainly no one else appeared disposed to raise the question.

Angus tapped his knife against his glass and said, 'There are just two notices this morning. Firstly I would like to say with regard to last night's happening, I hope no one of you will let that unpleasant and silly episode distress you. I'm sure there is a perfectly natural explanation for it.'

Theodora wondered what a perfectly natural explanation could be for a skull with a nail in it being found in a glass case under the biretta of a dead priest. Surely you couldn't have a real human skull floating about? Ought it not, if it were real, to be united with its body and then buried, preferably with the Church's rites?

Mrs Lemming creaked in her chair.

'Secondly, I have to tell you we shall have the honour of being joined at lunch by the Suffragan Bishop of Wormald, Bishop Francis Peake and his party.'

'What's his party?' asked Mrs Lemming who, with artistic dexterity, was dealing with a kipper.

'I understand the Archdeacon, Mr Gosh, and the Reverend the Honourable Martha Broad, who is now, of course, in priests' orders, will be with him.'

'No woman can be in priests' orders,' said Mr Clutton Brock, pausing as he conveyed mushrooms to his mouth. His eyes swept toward Theodora and then away again.

'Miss Braithwaite is in deacons' orders,' Canon Beagle stepped in.

Mr Clutton Brock looked as though he would say more and then decided against it. He took out a large, none-too-clean handkerchief and hawked into it. Mrs Lemming edged her kipper out of his range. Theodora reminded herself that bodies didn't matter, they were just impedimenta. Angus has said so twenty minutes ago.

'What brings them here?' Mrs Clutton Brock toyed with raspberries.

'I think, since you are our guests, it is only fair to share with you the possibility that St Sylvan's may not be able to continue as a pilgrimage centre. We do not make money. That is what the Bishop and his party are going to consider today.'

'What do they want to do with the place?'

'I think the diocesan authorities have it in mind to sell the site.'

'What will they sell it for?' Mrs Lemming was curious.

'I have heard it mentioned that it may be developed as a heritage centre.'

'Why don't they call heritage centres museums?'

'Lack of muses,' said Guy cheerfully.

'A saint's as good as a muse,' said Mrs Lemming who had, after all, been an Anglican all her life.

'What's the shortfall?' Canon Beagle could read a balance sheet.

'Half a million would be necessary.'

'We could pass the hat round. It was solvent in Bellaire's time.'

'Not entirely, I believe. It was Canon Tussock who put it on a proper footing.'

Guy raised his head from his task of spreading the maximum amount of marmalade on to a thick slice of wholemeal. 'They need to read the will,' he said and gave them all his wide-open smile.

The Right Reverend Francis Peake was not too sure how the Church differed from the world or indeed whether it should do so. '*We* set the agenda,' he was wont to tell diocesan training groups. 'But that agenda needs to be relevant, politically and socially relevant,' he said with emphasis, 'to the world's needs. We, the Church, have got to take a lead,' he would conclude often to applause.

He'd risen, he'd got his episcopal orders, partly by a judicious amount of boasting (high profiling, as he put it), partly by catching a doting old bishop's eye. The Bishop had been looking for a son that week and Francis had looked real son material. A youthful forty-year-old, he had retained, after some thought, the bodily movements of his undergraduate days. He could be found, on occasion, sitting cross-legged on the floor at the feet of men a little younger than himself. His fair hair crinkled like knitted wire over his large head, he wore his chin jutting forward to affirm his incisiveness. Nice teeth, nice figure, nice accent (which could go demotic if the occasion warranted it) recommended him. He talked of great events as though he had formed them and great men as though he knew them intimately. Few, after all, could check. It was amazing how far this could get you in the Church of England, ever ready to be impressed by the world. He'd a friend or two in the media, he'd told the old bishop. That had clinched it. The diocesan Bishop had followed his lifelong policy of picking men for office under him who were just slightly below par, who were not quite up to the job. He enjoyed their surprise and thereafter their gratitude and deference, both of which, as he got older, he found comforting. He had made Francis Peake his suffragan before his forty-first birthday.

Francis's greatest spiritual struggle thereafter had been whether or not to call himself 'Frank'. In the end he'd decided against it. He liked to have his cake and eat it, which might have suggested he should use both according to need and context. But he was a man of integrity. He'd stand by Francis. It was as well to keep in with the religious side of things.

Now, as he swung the wheel of his new Mondeo towards St Sylvan's he felt he was to face the first trial of his new strength. The place would have to go, whatever the locals thought. The road stretched ahead curving over the hills. The dry-stone walls hemmed in the sheep. The sun was up, the world was good. He should make St Sylvan's for ten-thirty. There would be time enough to say a pastoral word to the servants before the meeting.

He reviewed the field. There wouldn't be any problem from his fellow committee members. Angus whatshis-name was wet. He'd no clout. He didn't count. Not very senior in orders, he rather thought. Four or five years at most. He'd been a teacher or something dim before he'd been priested, he seemed to remember. As for Gosh, well, Gosh was just an evangelical barrow-boy. Full of enthusiasm and guitars and suchlike. Hopeless as Arch-deacon. Let the diocesan treat him like an office boy. So busy being jovially all things to all men, he'd no time to watch his back. That was a mistake in Peake's view. You'd got to be prepared to make enemies in this game. Standing up for the right and so on. Getting things done. Getting known for being what, after all, one actually was, pretty able, was what it was all about.

Bishop Peake put his foot on the accelerator to show how very powerful he was. The traffic was light. He'd passed one cyclist. He glanced in the driving mirror to see his new purple stock. It looked good; it suited him. He turned his thoughts to the coming meeting. He only needed to make three quick points, he reckoned: relevance, of course, money and er, redeployment. The lunch and back to report to and dine with the diocesan Bishop this evening.

Lunch with Martha Broad would be a bit of a pain. To say she really did come from a top family (Broads had had land at Rest since the Conquest), she was ghastly. Fat, for a start. Why did women let themselves go? And, frankly, women in orders! Of course in theory and in the modern world and all that but really there was no need for them. There wasn't anything they did as well as men. And as for them dressing up in clerical collars, it was just risible. He hadn't much time for them actually. He'd told his patron the diocesan Bishop. The diocesan, who entirely agreed with him, saw no reason, since he'd preferred Peake, not to punish him. 'The modern world,' said the old Bishop recalling something he thought he'd heard another bishop say in the House of Lords, 'is providing us with new challenges. Who knows where the Spirit may require us to go? The great question of our time for us is, can the Church catch the world up? We've got to do that if we're to lead it,' he had concluded oracularly. Francis hastened to agree with him. Actually he thought the old man was talking rubbish, beginning to lose his grip. Time he let younger and more able men step into the driving seats.

The car was new and clean, the upholstery well sprung; his driving gloves were smart. The document case and map on the seat beside him looked efficient and masterly. He felt he really did make a good bishop. The leadership role was so very important. Before the diocesan had picked him out at that fortunate dinner party, he'd sometimes feared he might not make it. Still, it had turned out all right on the night. Merit, of course, real quality, will out. But in the Church you could never tell. It was all rather chancy, not being able to apply for jobs, just having to wait around till you were invited and never really knowing what they were looking for. Must be terribly soul-destroying if you didn't have talent, mouldering in some obscure little country living burying unimportant people and marrying peasants.

He pressed the button which wound down the window and looked down over the chestnut forests. He was a town man, well, suburbs really, so the country was still a bit of an adventure to him. He hadn't quite got over how clean the air was out here. There were times when he felt almost attacked by it. He slowed down for the turning to St Sylvan's then braked. Slewed halfway across the narrow road was an ambulance. Or rather, it had once been an ambulance, now clearly it was something else. A multicoloured dragon's head had been painted across its back doors. One of these was open and from it spread a collection of dogs and children. The vehicle filled the road. It was impossible to pass.

Bishop Peake revved the engine of his new car. The dogs and children seemed not to hear him. He hesitated a moment and put on the handbrake and tooted on the horn in quite a friendly fashion. Still there was no sign of the vehicle moving. Peake felt a surge of irritation. Couldn't they see what he wanted? What on earth were they all doing? He framed his reproach. 'You do realise this is a public highway which it is an offence to obstruct.' Then he got out of the car and slammed the door to make them pay attention to him. He smiled commandingly at one of the children, a boy of about twelve. The boy was wearing a football shirt in Huddersfield Town colours and a pair of greenish cords rather too large for him, held up by washing-line. He was carrying something in his hand, Bishop Peake noticed. He looked more closely. It was a rabbit which the boy was holding by its back legs. From its mouth came the steady drip of blood on to the hot grey tarmac. A Jack Russell pirouetted round him to get at the corpse. The boy swung it high in the air to torment the dog. Bishop Peake stepped back to avoid being splattered by blood.

Irritation turned to anger. 'What is all this? What precisely is going on here?' Peake enquired.

The boy turned a blank face towards him. He seemed to see him from very far away. 'Blowy,' he said and managed to make the word sound sibilant.

In times of stress Francis Peake's hearing was not always reliable. 'What?' he asked. genuinely at a loss.

'Blowy,' repeated the boy.

'No it weren't,' said one of the girls with contempt. 'We skid, didn't we? Then the tyre go. That aren't wind. No way it was not.'

'Yah silly beggar. Blowy it was,' retorted her brother with spirit. 'Blowy the tyre.'

Bishop Peake felt he was losing control of the situation. 'Who's in charge here?' he demanded. He kept his smile in place but the tone was peremptory. Probably the boy was simple and if so he might be dangerous or anyway unpredictable. He looked at the dripping rabbit with loathing. The children gathered round him. There seemed to be a great many of them, surely more than the ambulance could hold. None of them looked clean. From the back row of the circle one of them pointed to the bishop's shirt. 'Nice shirt,' he remarked as though to an equal in sartorial affairs. 'Purple's nice.'

'Whose is this thing?' Peake gestured towards the obstructing ambulance.

'Blance is Gik's,' said the shirt expert.

'He's over the wall.' The girl flung her arm back over her shoulder.

Bishop Peake started towards the wall and then stopped. A tall male figure in a brown belted gabardine reared up from the other side. The man's face was long and tanned. He had a lot of dark curly hair which was neatly tied in the nape of his neck in a short queue. Peake formed the impression he was wearing no shirt under his gaberdine. The man gazed at Peake out of wide-set alien eyes. He spoke no word. Peake's temper snapped.

'I'm very much afraid,' he began dangerously, 'you'll have to move this thing at once. I have a very important appointment indeed, for which I am really rather late.' He shot his cuff to show his Rolex and tapped it lest the man should be deficient in the concept of time.

The man's eyes went from Peake's face to the watch. In a single movement he put his hand on the wall and vaulted over it landing upright immediately in front of and very close to Peake.

'Nice watch,' he said in an accent which was not easily assigned to any English county.

Peake could not bear the invasion of his space by the taller man. He stepped back. It was an unfortunate thing to do. His attendant crowd of children, including the boy holding the rabbit, had grouped themselves behind him. There was an anguished yelp from the Jack Russell as the Bishop's foot caught him. The dog abandoned the rabbit for the Bishop's leg.

No one seemed to feel it was the dog's fault. Two more dogs, much larger than the Jack Russell, fell out of the back of the ambulance and came to support the home team. The children cheered impartially. The brown gaberdine looked on as Bishop and dog fought it out. The noise rose to a crescendo until the man finally seemed to feel enough was enough. He gave a low whistle and the terrier rolled its eyes in his direction without actually letting go of the mouthful of trouser and flesh to which he had committed himself. At the second whistle, however, he disengaged and stood, his little feet splayed, his flanks heaving, his throat vibrating with growls.

Bishop Peake backed cautiously towards his brand-new car. With a final lurch he fell into the driving seat and banged the door shut. An inch of steel between himself and chaos revived the Bishop's courage. His mind turned to cliché as the needle to the North Pole. 'You have not heard the last of this matter, I can assure you. This is a very serious matter indeed. I have no intention of letting the matter drop. I know the Chief Constable very well indeed, as it happens.'

But the man in the gaberdine had lost interest. The chorus of children bore down upon the car. The boy with the rabbit held it up and swung it back and forth in front of the windscreen while the blood dripped on the bonnet. The Bishop reached for reverse.

CHAPTER SIX

From the Old Things to the New

'It's not being married to a clergyman that I find so unpleasant,' said Mrs Lemming. 'It's being married to Norman.'

Theodora wiped the sweat from her brow and plunged her fork into the end of the trench. She watched a wire worm slip adroitly between its prongs. Had it a mind or only behaviour? She looked up at Mrs Lemming who had a mind, indeed a troubled one. Society, a time when one gives out, Theodora reflected, solitude a time when one takes in. She had hoped for a rather larger dose of solitude at Rest. But after breakfast Mrs Lemming had followed her to the enclosed garden and tracked her down amongst the onion sets. Theodora had resolved to spend some time in useful unskilled physical labour. Since Tom Bough seemed not to object even if he evinced no actual enthusiasm, she had started out amongst the vegetables.

Mrs Lemming sat down on the bench beside the hose tap, embraced her knees and determinedly started to converse. Theodora had realised early in life that she attracted lame ducks as the magnet the steel. This was perfectly in order as far as she was concerned; if she could help, she would. It was just that at times she thirsted for a cessation of demands. She though of Geoffrey also about to embark on the perilous gamble of a lifetime's companionship with someone whom, surely, he hardly knew. How courageous, how rash the married were.

'You see he stops me speaking the truth. He simply makes it impossible.' Mrs Lemming was pressing on.

'How does he do that?' Theodora was interested in spite of herself.

'Well, now, of course, he has angina so that cuts out saying anything which could give him a sudden shock.'

Theodora wondered what this middle-aged woman could possibly have to say to her old husband, which, after thirty years of marriage, could cause his heart to palpitate.

'His ailments in old age chain me up as much now as his vocation did in his younger days. He uses both to stop me speaking.'

'How?' Theodora continued digging. She saw no reason, so far, to stop. Often people talked more freely if they felt themselves to be peripheral to your main attention. Mrs Lemming appeared not to resent the arrangement and pressed on with a fluency which made Theodora wonder if she had rehearsed.

'He uses fear, my fear of his panic. I sense panic behind his eyes when he's confronted with, oh, I don't know, ideas he can't understand, attitudes and values different from his own. He seems to feel that as a parish priest he ought to be omniscient. And of course he's not.'

Theoora was familiar with the syndrome. 'Priests are often seen as gods in their own parishes. We have great expectations of them. Too great, perhaps, for them to bear, too great for their own moral good.'

Mrs Lemming was delighted. Somebody understood what she was saying and didn't apparently, despise or judge her for saying it. She grew more confiding. With the detail born of suffering, she reviewed for Theodora's benefit the evasions she had noted over the years which her husband had adopted and refined to fend off the real world, that swirling chaos of the diverse and the unpredictable which threatened Norman Lemming's frail personality. She had watched him patronise and deflate, advise and rebuke as though from an immense moral height on matters far outside the sacramental. She had seen how he responded with elaborate and belittling courtesy to the laymen, and, even more, the women who did the work of the parish for him. She had listened to him preach Sunday after Sunday in the nineteenth-century pulpit in the nineteenth-century church stationed high above the congregation, so high that they had to tilt their heads back to see him. Thus elevated, already halfway to Heaven, he had preached sermons made up of quotations usually from the Bible. No one could criticise them. He rarely essayed comment above the most moralistic.

'I just can't understand,' Mrs Lemming cantered on, 'why they turned out to hear him. But, you know, he had a solid congregation for over twenty years. He wasn't kind. He wasn't concerned. Only frightened that anyone should find out he wasn't. He was like a parcel which no one had ever bothered to unwrap. Everyone assumed it contained the goods. I sometimes wonder if the congregation too feared that if they found there was nothing inside, it would be they who would be the poorer. We're all locked up in a self-deceiving game with Norman at its centre.'

Theodora felt she had heard this many times before, too many times for comfort. She recalled, as she always did on such occasions, her own excellent father's parochial practice just to remind herself that there were good parish priests, altar and office men, who performed competently and unobtrusively the duties of praying for Church and world. She turned her attention back to Mrs Lemming.

'And then, of course, there is the guilt,' Mrs Lemming was saying. 'The clergy seem to live in a sort of miasma of it. It's deadly. Norman plays a perpetual blame game to keep at bay the panic he feels. He's an absolute past master at making me feel guilty and half the time I don't know what I'm supposed to be guilty of. I must say there have been times when I've had murder in my heart.'

Mrs Lemming stopped and looked at Theodora. Had

she gone too far? What could this young woman know of such poison, forking and lifting onion sets with that easy regular strength born of healthy body and quiet conscience?

'I knew him, you know,' said Mrs Lemming suddenly changing tack.

'Who?'

'Tusk. Ben Tussock.'

'I thought you hadn't been here before.'

'No, no not here. Before here. Look.' Mrs Lemming scrabbled in her satchel. After a moment she brought out an enormous wallet-purse. Carefully she pulled out a photograph and handed it to Theodora.

Theodora wiped her hands on her denims, gingerly took the portrait and scrutinised it. It showed a man in his fifties, round-headed, cherubic about the eyes and chin, a generous mouth laughing and gleaming with life, a wide clerical collar finishing off, ruling a line under the confident features. It was Tussock all right, a lot younger than when she had seen him at school but unmistakably the same person. He was standing with a group of youngsters holding various gardening tools. The children's clothes dated it to the 1960s. The background was the front of the old kitchen.

'He could be great fun,' said Mrs Lemming unexpectedly. 'I met him once at a do at Cambridge with Norman. So, you see, I simply had to come to his own haunts when I heard he'd died.'

'I hope I make myself absolutely clear,' said the Bishop.

Martha Broad allowed her Biro to slide through her fingers. The fingers were large and white. They hung from her hands like a collection of parsnips. The hands finished off arms like hams which showed below sleeves rolled up in the warmth of the day. She wore a blue shirt with clerical collar, from which her round face emerged to hint at earlier prettiness. Her hair was cut short and brushed forward to form a thick grey cap. The room, the library of the guest-house, was hot. Outside Tom Bough's lawn-mowing activities could be heard as he brought the tractor up time after time to just outside the window and then like a cavalry charge wheeled it away at the last moment.

'I do think,' said Miss Broad, 'we ought to consider all alternatives before we take such an irrevocable step as closing St Sylvan's. Surely diocesan policy should try and take a long-term view not a short-term one based on—'

Bishop Peake leaned forward and cut across her before she had completed her sentence. The events earlier in his morning had rendered the Bishop less willing than normal to consider views different from his own. Now he said rapidly, 'Just two points, if I may. There can't be more than one alternative. That is what the word "alternative" means. As for diocesan policy, I think I may be allowed to be a little more knowledgeable than you in that area. I can assure you, I have the diocesan's confidence.'

He leaned back in his chair pleased with his performance. That one about 'alternative' was a good touch. It showed how sensitive he was to niceties of language. He'd had it pulled on him in youth and found it useful for cutting up the obstreperous.

Miss Broad flushed. 'Your remarks do not address the issues,' she said tartly. 'There are solid arguments which need to be looked at to do with what the Church takes to be its relation to the modern world. St Sylvan's is unique. If we are not to be driven mad by the world's evils, we desperately need special places to withdraw to, to find God in. It is the Church's function to provide such places. If the Church doesn't, no other institution can.'

She stopped. It was all so obvious to her. Why didn't the Bishop see it? The senior clergy had only enough nous to cling to their privileges. Their thinking was leavened by no sliver of common sense, their necks were stiffened with bigotry, and the empty space of their imaginations was populated only by visions of the House of Lords. She felt choked by her collar. There were times when she almost wished she hadn't taken orders. As a laywoman and a member of the most prominent family in the county, she had enjoyed a certain amount of influence. Now that she had taken orders she had become nothing more than a very junior member of a male hierarchy. All this rank-pulling sapped her energy.

The Bishop snapped shut his new leather notebook and reached for his smart leather document case. He saw no reason to answer the woman. He glanced at his watch and prepared to depart.

Angus looked at his agenda. He had written it on the back of an envelope of recycled paper. It read: 1. Prayers;

2. The function of pilgrimage centres; 3. The resources of St Sylvan's; 4. Identification of key issues; 5. Possible solutions. So far none of these items had been addressed. The Bishop had not worked to an agenda; he was against agendas. They seemed to him to be hostages to fortune, promises which it might be inconvenient for him to keep.

'I wonder if we aren't being too hasty?' Angus said cautiously, his Edinburgh accent sounding in every vowel. 'Many people have felt over a very long period of time that this is a place of great numinous power. It's not merely Christians in the orthodox sense who have benefited from the unique qualities of this place.'

The Bishop cut in and leaned forwards. 'I'm glad you take my point, Mr, er, Bootle. This place attracts the very worst elements in our society. New Agers, hippies, gypsies. I'm sure you realise from your own parish experience, on a smaller scale, that the Church has, above all, to be responsible and relevant. Those are the words I'd like you to take away from this meeting. Responsible and relevant. Hard decisions have to be made. We at the grass roots, at the centre of things, have to take the very widest view. It's a matter of stewardship and so on, you know.'

The Archdeacon cleared his throat. He felt he really ought to say something. He hated rows. He liked young people and simple music. In more adult contexts he was lost. His usual method in such cases was to wait until someone said something which he understood and then repeat it more loudly. He was less a speaker, more an amplifier. This economical technique had served him well in the Church. He tried it now.

'Relevance and responsibility,' he repeated. 'I think that puts it very well. Thank you for that, Bishop. What I feel we need to discern is, what is relevant? Where is the Spirit calling us on this one? Shouldn't the Church be helping people to practise the spiritual life? Recharge batteries and that. After all, if it's only a matter of money.'

The Bishop had had enough. It had been a long day. It had not started well. His ankle throbbed from the Jack Russell. He'd been very late. There hadn't been much in the way of lunch. Nothing to drink. He pushed the glass of springwater away from him petulantly.

'Money,' he said quietly to the Archdeacon, 'is very important. I don't think I should have to spell this out to you. The state of the Church's finances, the state of the country, Synod baying at our heels. All these make it absolutely imperative that we should shut up backwaters like this. The real world, the coalface is out there.'

'If money is so important,' said Martha Broad, 'why have the Board of Finance spent thirty thousand rebuilding the Dean's kitchen?' She could read a balance sheet and she reckoned she'd had more finance meetings than the Bishop had had hot dinners.

The Bishop reached for his briefcase from beside his chair. 'I am not at liberty to discuss a colleague's private affairs. I'm surprised you should not see the impropriety of such a remark. The site here will sell for half a million. Modern Heritage will be putting up a centre for Tudor arts and crafts. That will be a perfectly proper use which will maintain the spirit of the place. There'll be nature trails, tea towels, the lot. It could be an excellent asset to the diocese.'

The Archdeacon was not a courageous man. He lacked both information and principle. His mind, an infuriated junior cleric had said after failing to lodge new information in it, is so open it gapes. Nevertheless, he didn't care to be bullied.

'We've got an asset with the place as it is,' he protested bravely. He'd once been told that the secular world had skills the clergy needed but rejected because they were not of their devising. The Archdeacon wondered if it was these skills which he needed now. Words like 'planning', 'prioritising', 'monitoring' trailed slowly through his mind. But he knew his limitations: such concepts were not for him. Better keep to the tried and trusted. 'And I understood that the terms of the trust meant we couldn't sell up whilst there was income enough from capital to keep it going. I thought Tusk's money was coming here to swell the endowment.'

'You have been misinformed.' The Bishop was crisp and cheerful. He'd checked this one. 'Canon Tussock's money, quite properly, goes to the family.' He smiled at his adversaries. Early in his career the Bishop had learned to synthesise a smile out of the physical elements of smiling. The muscles round the eyes crinkled, the cheeks widened. Some unwary souls were lured by these purely physical manifestations into smiling back. Then the Bishop would dissolve the elements leaving them stranded. 'I think that concludes our business.' He switched off the smile.

'Would you care to stay for supper and compline?' Angus felt that, though the outcome of the meeting was so bitter, hospitality must not fail.

The Bishop looked at the springwater. 'I very much regret that is quite impossible. I am already engaged to dine with the diocesan.' He turned to the Archdeacon. 'The heritage people want to be in by September. I take it I can entrust the clearing up to you Jon.'

The Bishop was always magnanimous in victory. He signalled this by the use of the startled Archdeacon's first name. Before the latter could reply, however, the door opened without ceremony. The small figure of Guy Tussock dressed in black bathing-suit and trainers appeared on the threshold. He looked shyly round the clerical group and then said, 'I think you ought to come. There's someone dead.'

The woman's body lay beneath the deer's-head plaque beside the holy well of St Sylvan's. Water dripped from her denims and white shirt on to the stone flags. Her clothes were stained with mud and moss. One foot still retained a sandal, the other was bare. Her head was turned to one side and at the base of the scalp could be seen a long deep wound. Ruth Swallow's dark hair was heavy with water and a trail of water led back to the pool.

The Bishop, Angus, the Archdeacon and Martha Broad grouped round her.

Guy said, 'I pulled her out.'

The Bishop looked at the body with distaste. 'I think you see now how impossible it is for this to continue as

101

part of the diocesan structures.'

The inappropriateness of his response was allowed to hang in the air. Martha Broad looked up at the low cliff as though seeking comfort.

'An accident of this kind is very regrettable indeed.'

It was clear to all, except apparently the Bishop, that this was no accident.

Angus looked at the Bishop and the Archdeacon and then took charge. 'Would you be so kind, Mr Tussock, as to take your bicycle down to the village and phone for the police and an ambulance? And if you were to meet Miss Braithwaite and ask her to bring a blanket, it would be most seemly.'

The police came with exemplary speed. A sergeant and a constable scrambled up the narrow path and after one look raised mobile radios to mouths for reinforcements to cope with the event of death. The sergeant was young and efficient. He was not impressed by the Bishop or the clerical setting. He requested them to go to the guest-house and remain there until his superior officer could come and take statements.

The Bishop tried to set him right. 'I'm very much afraid it is quite impossible for me to delay my departure, Officer. I have a very important engagement this evening. I am dining with the diocesan Bishop. I really do have to get away pretty promptly.'

The Bishop's assumption that he was an exception to anyone else's systems was met with incomprehension by the sergeant. He was short with close-cropped ginger hair and long sideburns. His white nylon short-sleeved shirt was immaculate. He looked at the Bishop almost with pity. 'This is probably going to be a murder inquiry. No one can leave until the Inspector's done a preliminary. Now if you will kindly vacate the area immediately.' He spoke as though he were addressing a crowd through a megaphone. There was no sirring or pleasing.

The Bishop cleared his throat. 'I think I should tell you I know the Chief Constable very well indeed.'

Theodora, newly arrived with a blanket for the corpse, felt the tension of the party. Gently she placed the blanket over the body of the woman. The sergeant appeared not to have heard the Bishop. He set about putting white tape round the area. His constable, an older man with surprising grey hair visible beneath his cap, was more impressed by the row of clerical collars. Certainly he knew Martha Broad. 'If you wouldn't mind, Miss,' he said in fatherly fashion, 'I'm sure it won't be too long before the Inspector gets here and they'll make you right comfortable at the guest-house.'

Miss Broad stared down at the wet figure on the stones. 'Poor girl,' she said. 'Poor woman. Why on earth should anyone . . .?' She turned away and started heavily down the path.

Social and indeed religious skills to cope with murder are not often called upon. The gathering of pilgrims in the library was fraught. Theodora took a swift inventory. Mrs Lemming whom one might have supposed would be tearful looked alert, almost animated. Canon Beagle took out an office-book. Mr Clutton Brock sat in an armchair blowing his nose and mopping his brow, Mrs Clutton Brock stared out of the window which someone had closed as a sort of drawing down of blinds. Of Guy there was no sign. It was like a wake at which no one knew anyone. The four male clergy looked at each other. Since it had not apparently occurred to the Bishop, after a moment Canon Beagle, acting on his seniority, put down his office-book, cleared his throat and said, 'I think we need to pray for Mrs Swallow, for her family and her murderer, as well as for ourselves. Bishop would you care to lead us?'

The Bishop was loath to give up a leadership role but he had just enough instinct to know when he was out-classed. He did not know who Canon Beagle was but he recognised quality. The Archdeacon was invisible, Angus had the air of one swelling a progress. The women were not thought of.

Theodora admired Canon Beagle's liturgical range. They prayed for eternal rest, light and peace for the dead woman. They petitioned for the comfort of her family and friends. Nor did Canon Beagle duck the need for justice and repentence for evil-doers. They affirmed their sure and certain hope of the resurrection and dem-onstrated their unity in the faith by saying together the Lord's Prayer and the grace. St Sylvan might have been proud of him, Theodora thought, reflecting that fifteen hundred years ago the saint might have made the same prayers. As they prayed, so they bonded. At the finish they looked more kindly upon each other.

'Tea,' murmured Theodora and threading her way

round the assembled knees, made for the kitchen.

The kitchen was cool from its stone floor. Light slanted in from the low windows and the open back door. The paraphernalia of cooking for the evening meal was laid out, clean and ready for the cook who would not now return to it. On the table was a newspaper and a thick black-and-red notebook which looked as though it might contain accounts or receipts. Theodora saw the room for a moment as perhaps Ruth had seen it, as a domain, an important space where orderly, intelligent work was perfectly performed. It is no small matter to feed a dozen people excellently for week after week without fuss or waste. Why was it so despised, so taken for granted? Running a parish or a diocese, those more obvious mani-festations of power, required no greater talent. She felt a sudden kinship with the dead woman and an anger that she should be untimely snatched away. But then she realised she knew very little of Ruth Swallow. She'd spoken no more than a few words to her. Did she live in or come up from the village? Was she married or was her title of Mrs an honorific one from her job?

Methodically Theodora set about drawing water and assembling cups. The kettle, she noticed, was on a low light. As she was finishing, the door from the hall opened and Mrs Clutton Brock stood irresolutely in the frame. She gazed round the room before meeting Theodora's eye.

'I thought . . . I wondered if you . . . Victor likes camo-mile,' she brought out in a rush.

Theodora who had not forgotten this fact indicated

the separate arrangements she had made for the Clutton Brocks.

'Also,' Mrs Clutton Brock continued, 'I wondered if anyone had told Tom, Mr Bough. He would need to know.'

She hesitated and lingered. 'I think I might know where to . . .'

Even as she spoke, the light from the back door was obscured. Bough's figure, featureless with the sunlight behind him, seemed to tower above the two tall women. His presence, his emotion, flooded the room. In his hand he held a piece of oily rag and an adjustable spanner.

'Tom,' Theodora brought out, 'Mr Bough, Ruth, Mrs Swallow . . .'

'Where've they put her?' His voice was husky and furred. Theodora wasn't sure that she'd made out his words correctly.

'The well . . . the police . . .'

But the man turned and his footsteps could be heard gathering speed up the stone path. From the hallway behind them, came the noise of doors banging and a northern voice saying, 'Now then, Sergeant, look sharp. Where've you put them? I'll start with the top brass and work down the ranks.'

CHAPTER SEVEN

Let Him in Constancy

Frederika Bottomley, driving along the same road which Bishop Peake had traversed eight hours previously, likewise reviewed her career. She was finished. She'd decided that. This accident, manslaughter, murder, whatever it was, would be her last case. She had written her resignation and 1 September would see her free or on the scrapheap or whatever. She'd done thirty years in the force. As she watched the road unwind in front of her and remarked the pleasure of driving, she thought, I owe the force all the skills I've got. It's taught me everything I know: how to drive, how to write, how to speak, how to think. Was she grateful or not? At any event, the mark of the force was upon her. It would be interesting to see if there was anything more to her than what the force had issued her with. She'd need to discover that.

She'd given herself utterly, ardently to the work. It'd

been a hell of a struggle to stop being a WPC. She'd had to batter and push all the way. Nobody wanted her to succeed. Her family had been appalled at her choice of career. Her dad, a sergeant in the West Riding force for forty-one years, had told her, 'They won't want you, love. Just like you don't get men nursing, so you won't find women getting on in the force. You'll get hurt and not just by the villains.' Well, he'd been wrong, had Dad. Or partly. She had a friend who was a male nurse and people had stopped being surprised at him a decade ago. But the force was different, more resistant to change.

The radio-telephone on the dashboard showed signs of interrupting her thinking. She put a large heavy hand on it and it ceased to wheeze. She'd made Detective Inspector and she'd done it by being very persistent, and very loud and very thorough. She'd done her prep. on the clerical folks for example, as far as she could anyway. About the place itself, she'd have to do some finding out. She'd had to be quicker off the mark than her male colleagues and she'd been better at passing exams. But it had been a struggle. The top brass had resented it. They'd used every weapon to marginalise or patronise or downright bully her out of her rights. Scope for talent, that was all she'd ever wanted. If she'd been no good, she'd have left earlier or, more like, never started. But she was good, she knew that. They couldn't destroy her deep certainty that she knew what she was about. Why were they so bloody frightened all the time? She'd never got used to how scared they were. Anything new that they couldn't control or predict and the courage ebbed from them – and they reacted accordingly.

Why had she wanted to spend her life dipping into other people's when they were at their lowest, their worst point? Matt the nurse had asked her when she first met him '*I* can do something to help. Good nursing can save people's lives.' 'So can good policing,' she'd answered. 'People in a society like ours, in any society, have a right to safety and a spot of fair play.' But she'd answered by rote. Over the last few years she'd begun to doubt whether the desperate, the feckless or simply greedy could be contained. As she grew older and more senior every case she met seemed to be more complex than merely legal measures could deal with. Policing didn't change people's fundamental nature. She wondered if anything could do that.

If she'd lost her faith, it was time to get out while she was still ahead of the game. The pension was reasonable. At forty-eight she could still offer the world something. She'd have more time for life with Matt the nurse. She checked her watch. Fifteen minutes and she'd be there. She'd been surprised how ambition had drained out of her over the last twelve months since her transfer to the Wormald division. Perhaps it was the country air. Or possibly the type of crime. It was slower, she had to admit. Farmers fiddling the taxes, poachers after deer, a bit of drug-running and the usual car theft. But not like Leeds. Less racial tension, less violence. So a bit of proper crime would make a welcome change, nice thing to go out on.

She swerved round the corner for the last turn to Rest

and noticed in her noticing way the black tyre marks on the grey road surface and the pool of oil on the verge. Somebody'd had a spot of bother then. She put her foot down and raced on. Mustn't keep the clients waiting, dead or alive.

A final burst of speed brought her to the brow of the hill overlooking the valley of St Sylvan's. She slowed and took it all in. High up on the edge of the forest she could just glimpse the pediment of Broadcourt. Below that another stretch of forest and then one road in and one road out. Otherwise it would be approachable only on foot or by Range Rover or, of course, nowadays by mountain bike. It looked like paradise. The late after-noon sun caught the toy tower of the chapel. The old farmhouse and huddle of more modern buildings with the enclosed garden formed a graceful composition in the middle distance. A flag, at half-mast she noticed, waved over the guest-house. Wasn't there meant to be a pond or a spring or something, she'd heard, a holy spring? Where would that be? And what did they use it for? And who came? What did they do there apart, that was, from killing each other? The silence of the place came up and hit her as she leaned out of the window to check the notice-board. 'St Sylvan's at Rest, Pilgrimage Centre and Retreat House', it said, whatever that might be, God help.

One by one the little group of pilgrims assembled in the library were summoned to the dining-room next door by the ginger-haired sergeant. The Bishop went first and did not return. A little later the door of his car slammed loudly and the engine roared. There was a crunch of gravel and then silence. The Archdeacon plodded off and likewise did not return.

'Rather like being in the Ark,' said Canon Beagle as he set off in response to his name, bowling down the corridor. Fifteen minutes later he returned to share his experience with the rest.

'It's a bit like discovering God is a woman.' He was clearly in shock.

'I can't see why they can't send a proper crew or team or whatever they have. I suppose to the police the Church doesn't count nowadays.' Clutton Brock felt the insult. He glanced first at Martha Broad and then at Theodora, as though police policy on the employment of female labour might be their fault.

Theodora gathered the police inspector was a woman.

'Has she any clues?' Mrs Lemming asked. She lingered on the word as though it were not part of her normal vocabulary.

'Well, she wasn't sharing them with me if she had.'

'What did she ask?' Mrs Clutton Brock's question was unexpected, at least to Theodora. Mrs Clutton Brock evinced so little interest in her fellow human beings that any curiosity was remarkable. They all seemed brighter. Perhaps it needed a death to sharpen them into life.

'The thrust of her questioning was twofold.' Canon Beagle appeared to be enjoying himself. 'She wanted to know what I knew of Ruth, her background and so on and then she wanted to know where I was between three and five this afternoon.'

'And what did you tell her about Ruth?' Miss Broad

asked. Did she, Theodora wondered, know Ruth? The Broads were the big lay family in the district. They might well know something of the servants at the retreat house. Was the house perhaps on their land? She realised there was a great deal she didn't know. But then, she thought, why should I be interested? It's the police's job to get to this, not mine.

'I could tell them very little about Ruth, Miss Broad. Would it be that you could help them in that department?' Canon Beagle's tone made Theodora wonder if he was being disingenuous.

'Miss Swallow worked for us at Broadcourt for a number of years when she was in her teens. The Swallows were one of the estate families.'

Estate families, Theodora thought. It's feudal. Do people still go from village cottages to big houses as servants? Perhaps only females in remote areas, during times of recession.

'She came here just before Augustine Bellaire died,' Miss Broad said. 'In fact, I think she nursed him through his last illness.'

'Yes,' said Mrs Clutton Brock. 'That's right, she did.'

Martha Broad turned in her chair to fix her eye on Mrs Clutton Brock. 'Have we met before?' she asked, more county family than priest.

'It's possible,' Mrs Clutton Brock was no one's second in coolness.

'And where were you between the hours of three and five this afternoon?' Mrs Lemming turned to Canon Beagle as inexorably as a QC. The murder, its drama, had touched a well of energy and curiosity. Something tremendous and terrible had happened and she was not to blame. Perhaps it might be her turn to do some blaming. It would make a change.

'From three to four I slept in my room. From four to five I went for a spin round the estate,' answered the Canon equably.

'See anything untoward?' Mrs Lemming pressed him.

'Not a thing.' The Canon was emphatic.

Martha Broad got up suddenly and made as if to go out. Then she sat down again. 'I do hope someone has told Ruth's aunt. She'd be her nearest relation.' She turned to Theodora as though some explanation was necessary. 'Her aunt keeps the village shop. She's a very remarkable woman, Mrs Turk. She's entirely self-taught. Literature . . .' She trailed off as though the subject were beyond her.

Canon Beagle soothed, 'I think it's taken care of. I heard Angus asking the constable to do something with his mobile phone.'

'Well,' said Mrs Lemming, 'I at least know what I was doing between three and five this afternoon.' She looked round challengingly as though this might not always be the case. 'I was by the well working up my sketch.'

Mrs Clutton Brock looked up. 'But that's just the time, just the place when the girl was . . .'

'Until four-ish,' Mrs Lemming went on, 'then I went to find Miss Braithwaite. We had a *very* interesting conversation this morning.' She turned to Theodora to invite her collusion. 'I did so want to continue it. So I sought her out in the garden. But you weren't there.' She turned to Theodora. 'Where were you?'

'I may have been in the chapel,' Theodora admitted.

'For two hours?' Mrs Lemming was incredulous.

'Yes,' said Theodora. Had the woman no notion of what the religious life entailed? Possibly life with Norman had not led her down that path.

'Oh,' said Mrs Lemming, checked for a moment. 'And where were you two then?' She fixed her watery eye on the Clutton Brocks.

'I always practise after lunch if at all possible.' It was Mrs Clutton Brock who answered.

'Practise?'

'The cello.'

'And you?' Mrs Lemming transferred her interrogation to Mr Clutton Brock.

Really, thought Miss Broad with exasperation, the woman is shameless. What business was it of hers? What were the police for? She surely wasn't suggesting the Clutton Brocks had been ranging the domain bent on the murder of poor Ruth?

But Mrs Lemming had been sustained through a long dull marriage by curiosity. Now she had something to be curious about.

'I am my wife's severest critic,' said Mr Clutton Brock. 'She would not have achieved the eminence she has today without my efforts.'

Theodora looked across at them. They were seated on the sofa side by side but with a distance between them. Both sat bolt upright. Theodora searched her memory.

As though divining her thoughts, Mrs Clutton Brock said, 'I work under my own name, Lavinia Strong.'

Theodora placed her: middle-ranking quartet player, nineteenth-century stuff, some recent recording, mostly on the festival circuit. A travelling existence.

'Well,' said Mrs Lemming, 'that leaves Angus and the Bishop's party. I suppose none of you slipped out for a moment?' she enquired of Miss Broad conversationally.

'No,' said Miss Broad. 'And I don't think we should go on like this. It's tasteless and not our job. The police will see to it.'

'But someone killed Ruth Swallow.' Mrs Lemming was undaunted. She'd coped with tougher opposition than the Revd the Hon. Martha Broad.

'It doesn't have to be one of us,' snapped Miss Broad. 'There are all sorts of people who might have wandered through this place. It's very open. Indeed, that's just the point of a place of pilgrimage.'

'But what would have been their motive?' Mrs Lemming was undeterred. 'We need to keep that in mind, don't we?'

'We shan't know that until we know the killer,' said Mrs Clutton Brock.

'Ruth Swallow was pregnant,' said Mrs Lemming, playing her trump card.

'Are you sure?' Mrs Clutton Brock asked. 'I understood she wasn't married and the "Mrs" was an honorific title.'

'Who was the father?' Mr Clutton Brock joined in.

'Tom Bough, of course.' Mrs Lemming was triumphant.

'How do you know?' Miss Broad was less than pleased that an outsider should know more about the pilgrimage centre staff than she did. Really the woman was insufferable.

'I heard him talking to Guy,' Mrs Lemming answered without shame.

For a moment it looked as though Miss Broad would point out the iniquity of listening to other people's private conversations. Then she thought better of it.

'Where is Guy?' asked Canon Beagle.

'He never came back after Angus had asked him to ring the police,' answered Mr Clutton Brock.

Theodora had a wild feeling of their being in a game of Cluedo, only the body and the death and the loss were real. She badly wanted to get away and shake off this atmosphere of theatricality. She opened the door and stepped into the hall. From the library she heard the Scottish murmur of Angus answering questions. The grey-haired constable was standing, feet splayed, hands behind his back, in front of the hall door. As she approached he shook his head. 'Sorry, Miss. No one leaves until the Inspector's taken their statement.'

'I wondered if you and your colleagues might like some tea?' Theodora asked innocently.

The constable's ears pricked. 'That's right kind of you, Miss, if it wasn't too much bother.'

Theodora turned on her heel and made off down the corridor towards the kitchen. She had just reached the door when she heard her name called. The ginger-haired sergeant was holding a list. He had surprisingly donned a pair of steel-rimmed glasses in order to read it. It gave him a scholarly air at odds with the rest of him.

'Reverend Braithwaite? You're next.'

The dining-room had been rearranged to make it into an interview room. The light was behind the Inspector, the table was between them. Miss Bottomley was plain of face and plain of manner but the voice was low, northern, deliberate. The voice of someone prepared to take a lot of pains, to take all the time in the world.

'Miss Braithwaite? Now, put me right. Am I correct in thinking you're a priest?'

Theodora hated to disappoint but, 'No,' she said. 'No, I'm a deacon.'

'I'm flummoxed,' said the Inspector. But she didn't look it.

'It's sort of one below. As sergeant to inspector.'

'Right. But clergy at all events?'

'Right.'

'I've had', the Inspector consulted her list, 'a bishop, an archdeacon – new one on me that – and an incumbent. I think I'm getting the hang of it but I could do with a bit of help from an expert.' She looked at Theodora to see if the flattery would have any effect. Theodora moved not a muscle. 'Women can't be priests. Yes?'

'No. They can be. You've got one to come. Miss Broad's in priests' orders.'

'The Reverend the Honourable?'

'So I believe.'

'So why not you?'

Theodora wasn't going to go into all that. 'I'm hanging on as I am for a bit.'

The Inspector agreed to let that one go. 'Well now

Miss Braithwaite, my difficulty is that I'm a bit lost with all this clergy stuff. Frankly I don't know the systems, how it all functions, and I can't fit Ruth Swallow in.'

Theodora gave no help so the Inspector tried again. 'What I mean is, if you could give me any background information about the place or the people, it might make our work a lot easier.'

Theodora thought, she's floundering; she's out of her depth.

'To be honest,' Inspector Bottomley went on, 'I'm a bit out of my depth here. Have you, for example, formed any impression of the dead woman? What she was like, what her habits and character were, which might help us find out why someone might wish to kill her?'

'No,' Theodora answered. 'She seemed on the one occasion I saw her and Tom together to be relaxed, happy.' Theodora hesitated and thought of the kitchen with its workbox and waiting meal. 'She seemed suited to where she was and what she was doing.'

'Suited, eh?'

'I can't explain. She wasn't agitated, just, well, at ease. However, I know nothing of her background. Perhaps Miss Broad might be able to help you there. The Broads are the leading laymen round here. I gather she worked for them for some time.'

'You didn't know Miss Swallow when she was in Bradford doing some kind of course?'

'No, why should I?'

'You seem to have got around a bit; Oxford, Africa, South London. I looked you up.'

'Well I haven't ever got as far as Bradford.' So much, Theodora thought, for all that disingenuous stuff about not knowing how the clerical systems worked. Inspector Bottomley must have got at least as far as *Crockford*.

'You didn't know Mr Bough?'

'He drove us up. Apart from that, no.' Theodora wasn't going to dispense hearsay about Ruth and Mr Bough.

'You haven't been here before?'

'No.'

'And between the hours of three and five this afternoon you were where?'

Theodora provided her information. Inspector Bottomley seemed to find it less surprising than had Mrs Lemming.

'Anyone able to verify that?'

'No one at all,' said Theodora tranquilly. 'I was quite alone.'

'During your time here you haven't seen any strangers? Anyone not of the retreat?'

'No one.'

'Bishop Peake mentioned he'd seen a travellers' van,' Inspector Bottomley glanced at her notes. His actual words had been, 'I'm sure I need not tell you where to look for your killers, Inspector. I had to be very firm with them over one or two matters myself.'

'No, I've seen no one. We only arrived yesterday, Saturday.'

'Guy Tussock now. Some sort of relation to the founder?'

Theodora hated all this beating about the bush. Why

couldn't the woman ask straightforward questions of people who might be able to answer them instead of trying to lead one on?

'Not the founder. But certainly of one of the moving spirits.'

Inspector Bottomley realised she wasn't getting anywhere. She leaned forward and switched tack. 'What are places like this for, Miss Braithwaite?'

'They are here for the refreshment of the soul through the practice of prayer, reflection and physical work. They provide a context for people to become aware of the presence of God.'

'Not for settling old scores then?'

Theodora wasn't sure she'd heard the Inspector aright. 'I'm sorry?'

'What about the pool, the well?' The Inspector pressed on, whether on the same tack or another, she did not indicate. 'What's special about it?'

'I suspect its attraction comes not so much from its pious legend as from some deeper urge in us. Water is such a hopeful medium, don't you think? It seems as if it can make us quite different people, change us, make us better.'

'Reckon we could all do with a bit of that. Whose is it? Who started it off?'

'A Christian Roman soldier, Sylvanus, in the fifth century, made it famous by his noble death. Then a man called Bellaire resuscitated it as a pilgrimage centre just before the war and kept it going until another cleric, Canon Tussock, took it over in the sixties. He used the place rather differently.'

'How differently?'

'I think Bellaire believed in the pool, in its powers to focus the energies, almost to heal. I don't mean physical cures, more purging, integrating – all the things that religion's about. Tussock, on the other hand, just liked to get people together, perhaps to get them to like each other, a sort of microcosm of the Christian life.'

'Why should anyone want to live the Christian life?' asked Inspector Bottomley on the point of retirement.

'You deal with a lot of violence in the force, don't you? People at odds with themselves and so with each other. Nothing else can make an end of the violence.'

'How?'

'Just what you see here or rather just what I said. Use the traditional practices of religion, prayer, worship, reflection on Scripture, the support of the believing community, making an effort to change one's own nature which we call pilgrimage, the effort and example of Christ Himself.'

'I thought it was a matter of beliefs, what people think and they're pretty incredible, you've got to admit.'

'No,' said Theodora. 'No, not at all. It's not a matter of beliefs, not firstly. Firstly, it's a matter of doing certain things. People are religious if and when they *do* different things from unreligious people. Beliefs divide, practices unite. Both Bellaire and Tussock knew this in their different ways. Hence this centre. That's what places like this are for.'

'Has it ever been successful?' Inspector Bottomley asked dismissively. There wasn't a single category which she could make sense of in Theodora's explanation. Her own fault, she reflected, she'd asked the question.

'We've hardly begun to try,' said Theodora.

It was all very unsatisfactory. Inspector Bottomley looked through her notes. According to the preliminary report, Ruth Swallow had died at about five o'clock in the afternoon as a result of a blow to the back of her head. The wound had probably been caused by a stone being hurled with great force. She had been standing on the edge of the well looking down into it. The impact of the stone had knocked her into the water and rendered her unconscious. There was water in the lungs which suggested that she had been breathing when she entered the pool. Soon after five Guy Tussock, on his way back to his tent after a ride on his mountain bike, had found the body, pulled it out and given the alarm.

'Well Luff, lad, what do you think, eh?' Inspector Bottomley was not above exaggerating, even parodying her accent if she thought it served a purpose.

Luff looked through his own notes. He didn't reckon this woman Inspector, new to him and new to the division. He particularly hadn't liked that excursion into religion with that woman deacon or whatever she was. Religion left him uneasy. All right for women but the rest of us have work to do. But Inspector Bottomley was known to be a canny lass. He might learn a trick worth two if he kept sharp. He intended to make the plainclothes lot if it killed him. He shuffled his papers. 'I take it we can write the Bishop's party off, Peake, Bottle, Broad, Gosh. Pity really. That Bishop's a right superior beggar.

If that's religion, you can stuff it.'

'Can't write it all off like that. There are some very nasty senior coppers. Doesn't mean there's no point in police work in general. While they have the sterling worth of the likes of you and me, Sergeant.'

'I thought it was supposed to be different with religion. That woman . . .' He searched his list.

'Broad?'

'No, the other one, Braithwaite. She was saying the same as me, if I followed her. She said it's what you do that matters. You can see what that Bishop does. He's a liar and a boaster and a bully.'

'Doesn't make him a murderer, Sergeant.'

'Does after a fashion.'

'Quite a little philosopher. I didn't know you felt so strongly.'

'Had one of them as my first sergeant when I joined the force. I'll never forgive him. D'you think he does know the Chief Constable?'

'Doesn't matter, does it? Chief Constables like crimes solved, showing on their statistics. Chaps in purple vests won't do that for him. However, doesn't get us any forrader in the case of Miss R. S.'

'What about the Bishop's suggestion of travellers?' Luff knew where he was with travellers.

'There could have been a van through. I saw a bit of oil on the road as I came up. Bootle was saying they gather here about now for St Sylvan's day, end of this week apparently. Doesn't make them killers, living in a van.'

'Untidy. Leave a lot of dirty litter, gypsies.'

'What would be the motive though?'

'Could be a nutter?'

'Plenty of those about. Still, you're right, of course. We ought to have a word. See if you can pick 'em up. A van with a dragon on the back, your favourite Bishop said. Shouldn't be too difficult to spot. How about scene of crime?'

Luff felt he was getting on well. The woman wasn't that bad after all. She'd taken his suggestion seriously. 'Nowt. Tyre marks all over the place from that Canon's wheelchair. Yesterday, today. Who knows? And that lad's mountain bike the same.'

'What about this here Canon? Canon Beagle?'

'He's not got much of an alibi.' Luff peered through his spectacles. ' "At the time in which you are interested I would judge I was somewhere near the south door of the chapel", is what he said. In fact, he hasn't got anyone who can corroborate that.'

'Anything strike you about the Canon, Sergeant?'

Luff reflected. 'Powerful bloke,' he said after a minute.

Inspector Bottomley nodded. 'According to their book of words,' Inspector Bottomley tapped her copy of *Crockford's*, 'he had a half-blue for the decathlon in 1934.'

Luff didn't know which impressed him more, her having done her research in some book he'd never heard of or the fact that his own father hadn't been born in 1934. 'It's a hell of a long time ago,' was all that he could manage.

'Correct me if I'm wrong, Sergeant, but one of the events in which you have to excel in order to compete in a decathlon is putting the shot, yes?'

'Right,' said Luff. 'That's right.'

'Good practice for hurling rocks accurately sixty years later, would you say?'

Luff couldn't make out if she was laughing at him or not. 'He's got a hell of a pair of shoulders on him still,' he said safely.

'Motive?'

'Nay.' Luff shook his head.

'Enough of the Canon. But we'll keep him on the list just the same. How about the women, Mrs Lemming?'

'She said she was at the pool until four then went in search of the Reverend Braithwaite but didn't look in the chapel.'

'So neither she nor Miss Braithwaite have anyone to corroborate them. Still, I don't see Mrs L. having the physical strength.'

'She's venom enough to though,' Luff said with admiration. 'And the Braithwaite woman's athletic enough to nip up to the pool, hurl the rock and get back to the chapel sharpish, given she went there at all.'

'Do you see her killing Ruth Swallow?' asked Inspector Bottomley.

'Lot of strength there,' Luff admitted. 'But sort of a different kind.'

'Moral, perhaps,' said the Inspector ruminatively, 'or possibly,' a new thought struck her, 'spiritual?'

'Could be right.' Luff wasn't too eager to stray down

unfamiliar paths. 'What about the other woman, Mrs Clutton Brock?'

'Hers and her husband's account support each other for what it's worth. Practising their cello until twenty past five. He says,' Inspector Bottomley flicked through her notes, 'at a quarter to five he looked out of the window and saw Bough walking away from the house.'

'Did Mrs C. B. see that?'

'Not according to my notes,' said the Inspector. 'On the other hand, why should he say he had if he hadn't?'

'Might be giving someone an alibi?' Luff was puzzled.

'How long does it take for someone to get from here to the pool?'

Luff was extremely proud of himself. 'I ran it as fast as I could. It takes eleven minutes. It's the bit at the end when you have to get round the trees and rocks. They act as a sort of barrier really between the pool and the rest of the grounds.'

'So Both Guy and Bough might still have made it. I mean we can't time the death to anything like five minutes.'

'Well, we know she was dead by five past because Guy says he pulled her out at that time, dead.'

'I wish to God we'd got Guy's statement,' said Inspector Bottomley, arranging her notes in alphabetical order. 'Where was he before he went to the pool?'

'He had his tent pitched above the pool. He might have been going back there.'

'He'll not get so far. Not even on that bike of his. I've got a call out to all divisions.'

'Let's assume for the moment that it's intrinsically

unlikely that the same man should both discover and bring to the attention of the police a murder, and perpetrate it himself.' Inspector Bottomley was didactic.

'Well,' said Luff, 'there was that case in Farsley couple of years back.'

'Yes, yes, I know,' Inspector Bottomley was not going to be cheated of her hypothesis. 'Nevertheless,' she went on heavily, 'let's just suppose for a minute that everyone's telling the truth. They're religious people after all. Where does that leave us?'

'Tom Bough.'

'He'd have a motive, I suppose.' Inspector Bottomley was reluctant. 'That stuff about Ruth having his child which Mrs Lemming went on about. Still, there are quicker ways of terminating an unwanted pregnancy than killing the mother.'

'Perhaps', Luff waved his hand in the direction of the crucifix, 'she wanted to keep the kid. Maybe she was religious.' Luff thumbed through to find his notes. 'He says here he left Ruth washing up after lunch and went down to his shed to mend the clutch on the minibus. He came out about half-past four and went back to the kitchen looking for some tea. He noticed that the tray was laid for the guests' tea but no sign of Ruth. He put the kettle on and went in search of her in the vegetable garden. When he didn't find her he came back to turn the tea off and heard the police car. He went into the kitchen and met Miss Braithwaite and Mrs C. B. who indicated something to do with Ruth was "out of order". His words.'

'It's a hell of a long time to be looking for someone

in a small vegetable patch from, say, twenty to five to half-past.'

'It's not a satisfactory story, would you say?'

Luff was getting into the style of conversing with a colleague rather than just waiting to be prompted, Inspector Bottomley noticed. The lad was learning. If we don't look out, we shall have a rational, mannerly police force. Then where should we be? 'Look,' she said, making up her mind. 'Its not the strongest case in the world but Bough is clearly the most likely. He's physically strong, he struck me as capable of having a temper and the tale doesn't quite stand up. We'll have another go at him in the morning.'

'Shall I check to see if he's got any form?' Luff said on inspiration.

'Right.' Inspector Bottomley looked at her watch. 'Doctor's full report won't be here till ten. How about the press?'

'Not a dickie bird owing to this place not being on the phone.' Luff was gleeful.

'Won't last,' said Inspector Bottomley dourly. ' "Murder at the Holy Well" might make the nationals in a quiet season, like what we've got. I'll give you a press release. We don't want anyone compromising the case by being taken for a ride by clever reporters, do we?'

Luff supposed she meant that an inexperienced copper could give away too much. But somehow he didn't resent this slur on his professionalism. She wasn't out to put him down.

'I think you'd better go back to base and put in the paperwork. Tell them we shall want some more mobile phones and another computer. Can't have you exhausting yourself with all this handwriting, eh, Sergeant?'

'Are you staying on here, Inspector?' He was damned if he'd call her ma'am.

'Aye. I'll stay overnight. And, what's more, Sergeant, I am going to take the opportunity to immerse myself in the religious life.'

'Brethren, be sober, be vigilant, for thine adversary the Devil goeth about like roaring lion seeking whom he may devour, whom resist, steadfast in the faith.'

Theodora heard the ancient words with thankfulness. Normally the late evening office of compline was her favourite. The end of the day prefigured the end of life, all tasks accomplished, all passions spent. Today had not been like that. The disfigured features of the dead woman were vivid in her memory. She felt no ability to concentrate herself in prayer to dispel her distress. Why, she wondered, did she find the spectacle of a woman's death so much more horrifying than a man's? She had after all seen a fair amount of death in the course of her life. Africa had been full of it. Betterhouse provided its quota of such violence. Perhaps it was because, on the whole, women did not themselves kill quite so often as men. Perhaps too, she admitted to herself, it was the completion of the role of victim so often offered to and taken up by women. They, we, shouldn't do it; we shouldn't let ourselves become victims. It's not fair on

our killers. She felt irrational anger at Ruth allowing it
to happen. She should have been stronger, quicker, more
resourceful, she thought.

She glanced round the tiny chapel. It was lit only by
six candles. Two were on the altar, two each on the
pews which faced each other, monkish fashion, across the
choir. From time to time the shadows leapt into dragon
and serpent shapes as the draught made the flames
gutter.

'Before the ending of the day, O Saviour of the world
we pray.' Angus's voice was steady and resolute in the
face of encroaching darkness. In the pew opposite, Theodora could make out Mrs Lemming. She had her eyes
fixed on the east window and was making nervous scrab-
bling sounds with her hands in the service book. Next to
her was Mrs Clutton Brock, her head bent, her figure
still, but not, Theodora thought, with the stillness of
contemplation, rather a sort of rigid tension, like one
of her own stretched bowstrings. Below them, from his
chair parked at the chancel steps, Canon Beagle's strong
voice made the responses. At her back. Mr Clutton
Brock could be felt rather than heard since he uttered
no response other than to sneeze from time to time.
Down towards the west door she thought she could make
out the bulky figure of Tom Bough standing still and
soundless. To his left and behind him, Theodora was
surprised to detect Inspector Bottomley. What did the
woman want? Was she spying on them?

'Hide me under the shadow of Thy wing,' Angus said
in his pleasant baritone.

Who had killed Ruth and why? Was it linked with the skull beneath the biretta? Theodora's attention wandered back to the day's events. The Inspector had not asked about the incident. Perhaps she had not been told about it. She rather pitied the woman, who would find it difficult to break into a terrain as fenced about as a set of Anglican clerics and their retreatants. But then perhaps Ruth's death had nothing to do with the place or its people. Most killings had their origins in the past history of the victim and of that she knew, as yet, nothing.

The light had lessened as the liturgy progressed. Now there was nothing but darkness and the six candles. Angus had asked her to pray for the final blessing. 'In the circumstances,' he'd said. He meant but did not say, because it's a woman who has been killed. Accordingly, as the office drew to its end, Theodora stepped forward. But before she could form her prayer, the door at the west end of the chapel swung open. A gust of air took out one of the candles and a sudden scream from Mrs Lemming broke the silence. All faces turned towards the west end and the sudden inrush of warm air. Theodora made out a figure in a cope standing for a moment framed on the threshold of the chapel door. Then almost at once the shadows of the candles settled and the door swung to. The figure was no more seen. There was a sound of running footsteps as Inspector Bottomley swung at a good pace down the aisle and wrestled with the unfamiliar fastenings on the chapel door.

'It's Father Bellaire,' Mrs Lemming hissed, 'dead these seven years.'

131

Theodora prayed the blessing in spite of all, to wind up the spell of the liturgy.

CHAPTER EIGHT

Broken Peace

The day after the murder the path from St Sylvan's to
the village of Rest was crowded. A police van and a
couple of private cars had already passed Theodora as
she made her way towards the village after breakfast. So
that was the end of the peace and solitude of the place.
It didn't feel like a Monday morning. It didn't feel like
anything. She had slept shortly and badly. What was
happening at this place? This holy place? Say the biretta
and skull incident were linked to last night's appearance
of the cope at the chapel door, and both to the murder of
Ruth Swallow. What message was being sent and by
whom and to whom? Both biretta and cope belonged to
Father Augustine Bellaire. Would the biretta's place
under the skull suggest that Father Augustine was being
connected with death, the nail that the death had
deserved? But that was idiotic. The man had died with

his boots on at a ripe old age. All deaths of that kind were deserved. They have no menace or tragedy in them. Theodora was not a solver of crosswords, she didn't care to be taunted with clues. The thing that was clear was that the only way to restore St Sylvan's to its peaceful state was to find out who killed Ruth and why, and who played silly beggars with skulls and copes.

Theodora dodged round a couple of sheep straying down the middle of the path who seemed not to know where they were but were bent on eating as much as they could before being returned to the rest of their kind. Just one more sign of chaos and stupidity, thought Theodora testily, as they went through the rigmarole of being terrified at the approach of a human being and bolting another twenty yards down the lane. There were no hypotheses she could frame until she knew much more about Ruth. The best source of that information would be her aunt, Mrs Turk of the village shop. She would also need to know about the history of St Sylvan's as a pilgrimage centre. She'd seek help there from Canon Beagle, he looked sane enough, and perhaps Lavinia Strong, Mrs Clutton Brock. About Mr Clutton Brock she would have to penetrate Mrs C.B.'s immense reserve to get any information there.

Then, of course, there was Guy. Why on earth had the lad disappeared? He must realise that he would be needed for inquiries and would be caught in due course. Would he have killed Ruth? Whyever should he want to? She rather wished she'd been more forthcoming to Inspector Bottomley. There was information she could do with which only the police would have. When precisely had Ruth been killed and had it been the head wound or had she drowned? What about Tom Bough? What did the police think about him?

Theodora stepped down into the dimly lit space of the village shop. There wasn't much room and what there was was further confined by a couple of nets of spinach and open sacks of potatoes and beans. From one of the latter, as Theodora stumbled against it, there rose a huge black shape which changed slowly into an affronted cat. It glared for a moment and then sat down again folding its feet deliberately beneath itself and taking up its stance as though waiting to be entertained.

Theodora looked around. The window, which did not display goods for sale, was nearly at floor-level and kept out the light by being papered with advertisements for teas of a make with which Theodora was unfamiliar, though whether by virtue of their age or their northern provenance, she could not tell. This arrangement left the upper part of the room in darkness. She had entered with bent head and wondered if she dare stretch up. A thin pipe ran out of the back of the shop and ended in the gauze bulb of a gas mantle. It was not, however, lit. Dangling from a beam not too far above her was a string of onions and a swatch of bacon. The place smelt strongly of spices, apples and cat. To her left, however, unexpected in this 1900s interior, she noticed wedged up into the corner, a useful-looking full wine rack. Of the proprietor there was no sign. As she had entered a bell quivered on a spring but this had produced neither noise nor occupant. Theodora waited. The cat waited. Then a voice, 'They do say that the chemicals used to decaffeinate coffee are more harmful to us than the caffeine in the original liquor.'

Theodora peered into the shadows whence came the voice. Slowly as her eyes got used to the dimness she made out an immense shape which she had at first taken to be part of the furniture. The voice from the shape was soft, modulated, with a northern accent but somehow cultivated. The shape leaned forward over the counter and said quietly, 'Would it be Miss Braithwaite, in deacons' orders, from St Sylvan's?'

'Yes,' said Theodora. 'Yes, I am.'

'Rosanna Turk,' said the bulk and an enormous arm extended itself across the counter. Theodora met a firm grip.

'I'm so very sorry about Ruth,' said Theodora.'

There was a pause then Mrs Turk said, ' "I have discussed, we are but dust, and die we must." But,' she added, 'I look for retribution.' She half-rose out of her seat, fixed her eye on Theodora and said, 'St Sylvan's had much to answer for.'

Theodora thought, there's no point in beating about the bush with banalities which Mrs Turk would scorn. 'I was wondering', she said, 'if you could help.'

'The bacon's good,' said her hostess. 'It will not exude large quantities of water when fried. It has been properly cured by Mr Rowbottom of Broadcourt Home Farm, whose family have done it for six generations. The cheese is better,' she went on. 'I have the same factor as Fortnum's for cheddar. They approve my conditions for keeping it. It is strange, do you not think, Miss Braithwaite, that appreciation of fine foods and wines (my own selection is not negligible) – ' she waved a hand at the rack – 'on the part of the newly rich, outstrips their knowledge of the culture and values, the literature, upon which these products were originally based?'

'I've never thought about the connections between food and literary values,' said Theodora with honesty. 'I think I may have been brought up to suppose high thinking went with plain living.'

'There's plain and there's junk; as in food, so in morals. My poor niece now . . .'

'Your brother's child?' Theodora hazarded. It was time, she felt, to get down to brass tacks.

'I shall tell you all you need to know. But first we need refreshment.' Mrs Turk consulted her watch. It was a delicate gold piece pinned on her chest like a medal. Her double chins made consultation something of a dramatic gesture. She had to lower her shoulders and extend her neck upwards, then bend her head from the poll like a well-made horse. With surprising fleetness of foot, Mrs Turk stepped backwards into the shadows and opened a matchwood door behind her. Theodora had a brief vision of a parlour complete with rag rug, china dogs and a mantelshelf clock. She waited. There was a sound of thunder and a juddering of pipes, then the high whirring of a coffee grinder and a smell of fresh coffee. A few moments later Mrs Turk put down a tray with a Rockingham coffee pot and two matching cups on it.

'Draw up,' she invited Theodora. 'Turf Rodney off. She's much too possessive about those beans.'

Theodora looked the cat in the eye and thought she wouldn't care to mix it with Rodney, whatever its sex. Instead she pulled up a small wooden chair of the sort sometimes found beside tennis courts for linesmen.

The coffee was full and rich.

'Packed with caffeine,' said Mrs Turk.

'I need to know about Ruth, Tom Bough and St Sylvan's.' Theodora set out her agenda. 'I have a feeling her death is more connected with the place than with anything else.'

'My niece is the daughter of my only sister, Naomi. Of that there is no doubt. About her father, however, there is less certitude. You may think', she leaned over her coffee cup towards Theodora, 'such a question is *nihiliflocci*.'

Theodora had to admit to herself that that had not been her thought.

'But I assure you,' Mrs Turk went on, 'in a community of this size and composition, it mattered out of all proportion who one's father was. And thirty years ago yet more. Of course, the Swallows, my father's family, were an old St Sylvan's family. We were farriers here since the Civil War. So Naomi and I were people with a place. It was, therefore, a disaster for her when she became pregnant without first having taken the precaution of marriage.'

'When would this be?' Theodora enquired.

'Ruth was thirty. Not far, I would judge, from your

own years. Naomi conceived in the summer of 1962 whilst helping with the domestic arrangement of St Sylvan's for its annual feast day.'

'Did she not divulge the father's name?' Theodora realised she was picking up Mrs Turk's diction.

'We were very close as sisters. I was the elder by only two years. We kept little from each other but this she would not tell me. Whether she told anyone else, I do not know. She was extremely distressed. She had wanted children. The domestic life appealed to her as it does to many women,' Mrs Turk extended her broad forgiveness to those of her sex who were so mistaken as to pursue such a line, 'but not quite in the way it happened.'

'What happened?'

'My sister had the child away from home, itself a departure from the custom of our family, in hospital in Bradford. Then she died the following year.'

'So who . . .?'

'There was no one else but me. My husband had departed for more delectable pastures after three years of our union. I had not been blessed with children, so I had no objection. It seemed to me I might have the pleasure of childrearing without the physical and mental pain of birth. Certainly I had the pleasure of educating Ruth. She is,' Mrs Turk stopped and frowned, 'she could have been a good scholar.' Mrs Turk used the old-fashioned word. 'She was well grounded in English and French literature. She was mathematically competent.' Mrs Turk stopped and fixed her eye on Theodora. 'Have you the learned tongues?' she enquired.

It was rare, Theodora realised for anyone to actually value such knowledge nowadays. 'Yes, a smattering,' said Theodora who had a first in classical mods.

'You are to be envied. Such riches,' said Mrs Turk. 'I have had to teach myself, which is laborious and lays one open to shaming lacuna and mistakes.' She cocked an eye at Theodora. Theodora had not detected any mistakes anywhere in Mrs Turk's eloquent discourse and she didn't in any case judge people's moral worth by that means.

'What about Ruth?' Theodora pressed her.

'Ruth. As is often the case with parenthood, I believe, she took against her teachers and wanted nothing more than to follow the domestic life. I thought if one were going to do nothing but cook, then at least she should be trained for it. But she wouldn't. She started a course in Bradford. Then when Humphrey Broad had his last stroke, she came back and went to Broadcourt to nurse him. When he died – I do not think there was any causal connection – she took on the domestic management of St Sylvan's. An utter waste. As it had been with her mother before her.'

'She seemed to me,' Theodora said, 'to have made a complete, integrated, almost religious life out of it. There was something nunlike about her. She grew much of what she cooked and what she cooked was of its kind excellent. And after all if she was happy . . .'

Mrs Turk snorted. 'There are noble sources of happiness and banausic ones. She would be happy taking the whole day making a cherry pie, taking the stones out, cooking the pastry. She did everything so slowly. I can't say how irritating I found it.'

'Was she going to settle down and marry Tom Bough?'

'I believe that was her, if not his, intention.'

'Was he not for settling?'

'Oh, he's a good enough man is Bough. There've always been Boughs at Rest.' Mrs Turk seemed to estimate moral worth in terms of residence. 'It's just that he's fifteen years older than she. Literature is littered with the folly accruing from such arrangements.'

'And her death?' Theodora pressed her. 'How might that be related?'

'I always thought her wish to return to St Sylvan's was *au fond* a wish to find out who her father was.'

'Did she care that much?'

'She liked the idea of a family, brothers, cousins, that sort of thing. She wasn't mystical, blood bonds and all that, just, well, just domestic.'

Theodora considered. 'Wouldn't there have been records of who visited St Sylvan's at the time of Naomi's affair? Couldn't Ruth, if she'd really wanted to, have found out, eliminated the possibilities?'

'I don't know whether Bellaire was the sort of man who kept records. He always struck me as rather wilful, just an autocrat who happened to have taken up religion, not a religious man who happened to be autocratic. But perhaps I am wrong. I am not myself *croyante*.'

'But if Ruth was that keen? If she'd started asking around about her father, and if she had found out and that knowledge was inconvenient for someone?'

'Yes,' said Mrs Turk. She sounded suddenly tired and dispirited. The *élan*, the bravura had gone. 'Yes, I think she may have found out who her father was. I don't know how. But she came down to see me on the Friday night, the night before the new set of pilgrims, of whom, I suppose you are one, arrived on Saturday. She said, "I think I've got some relations coming on Saturday. Some of my dad's people.'

'She mentioned no names?'

'None. She was as close as ever her mother was.'

'It's a beginning,' said Theodora. 'It's better than nothing.' It's better, she thought, than the police have managed. 'Did she say anything else?'

'Just one more thing. When I asked her who she thought was coming, she said, ' "I am the mower Damon known Through all the meadows I have mown." "

Mrs Turk turned her eye on Theodora. 'Now what would you make of that?'

Theodora felt it was some sort of test. 'A metaphor for death or for sexual conquest.'

'Take it whichever way you like,' said Mrs Turk.

At nine-thirty on Tuesday morning in the library now doubling as the incident room and filled with the desired computer, phones and filing cabinets – Inspector Bottomley and Sergeant Luff pored over the doctor's report, the ballistic expert's report, their case notes and the statements of all relevant parties. They'd interviewed the aunt, Mrs Turk. She had told them no more than they already knew. At ten-thirty Inspector Bottomley had Tom Bough in again and at ten-fifty she invited him to accompany them to Wormald police station to help them with their inquiries. He'd not helped himself. He'd been truculent, monosyllabic, turning his head away from each of them in turn like a horse refusing a jump. Luff had been through the records. Yes, he'd done eighteen months for GBH. It had been fifteen years ago. He'd been no more than a lad and in drink at the time. Frederika offered the medical report which showed Ruth was due to have a child. Was it his child? He bloody well hoped so. He'd stopped, realising there would be no child. No Ruth. He'd shut his mouth then and would say no more.

Inspector Bottomley told Luff she didn't like the look of the case at all. She badly wanted to question Guy and she wanted the travellers' van found – and what was Luff doing about it? Luff admitted both seemed to have vanished off the face of the earth. Inspector Bottomley made disapproving noises. But in the absence of both and given the balance of probabilities, she felt she could do no other than follow her training. Luff had been quietly delighted. It was his first proper murder and if it was that easy he didn't doubt he'd make Detective Sergeant by the New Year. He had nous enough to keep his thoughts to himself.

'What do you want me to do, Inspector?' he asked to keep his superior in countenance.

'Stay on here and get this lot cleared up. Give the press that statement I prepared and keep them happy and ignorant. I'm going down to Wormald with Bough and if I don't get what I want, I'll be back tonight and I want to find it all nice and quiet and shipshape here. This place isn't meant for noise and flashbulbs.'

The guest-house was, by its own standards, pandemonium. Canon Beagle bowled his chair down the corridor scattering youthful police and reporters to left and right. Those who had known him in his younger days would have recognised a fly-half of international standard making for the three-quarter line. His eye glowed red. He uttered not a word. He knew what he was after. He made for the library at a good pace. Outside he braked and accosted a surprised policeman by saying, 'Can I have a go on your machine?'

'Eh?' said the startled constable.

'Your machine. Your portable phone.'

'Well, er, I . . .' This was outside the youth's experience.

'I need to get hold of Angus, Mr Bootle. He's at his vicarage. Wise man. It's not that I couldn't do it, make the journey. But I need him now.'

'If it's important, sir, could I help you?' He was a country youth and had not learned to be disobliging.

'It is important but I don't think you can help, Officer. It's a pastoral matter,' he explained. 'The Church.' He touched his collar.

'Ah.' The constable hesitated. He wasn't sure whether he should be impressed or not. He didn't really know terribly much about the Church. It hadn't impinged on him much before this interesting débâcle.

'Look, show me how it works,' Canon Beagle invited. It was an inspiration. Who can resist showing off knowledge?

'You just . . .' said the constable.

'Marvellous. Thanks very much,' said Canon Beagle and clicked Angus's number.

'Hello, Bootle?' Canon Beagle made no concessions to modern familiarity. 'About that skull business.' He glanced at the constable who was hovering. 'I think I should have a word. Can you come up? After your sick communions? Right. I'll be by the well.' He glanced at the policeman. 'More private. Dinky little beasts, aren't they? Thanks awfully, Officer.'

The constable looked as though he thought he ought to say a word but couldn't think which one. The Canon swivelled round him and made for the well. There was a lot of white tape round it but no actual policemen. Canon Beagle held up the tape with one hand and bowled his chair through with the other. He made the terrace and posted himself in the shade of the ilex. The sun still shone. That made three days in succession. It was warmer than it had a right to be in Yorkshire at any time of year.

Once in situ, Canon Beagle reviewed his knowledge. That skull business, had it anything to do with the girl's death? One thing was certain, Bough hadn't been involved in that. That sort of jokiness didn't fit in with what he'd seen of Bough at all. He thought again about the words he had heard through his window. He'd talk it over with Angus and see what the lad thought. He folded his hands on his chest. After a moment or two he tipped his panama over his eyes, released his teeth and let his jaw drop. Mrs Lemming, who had likewise dipped under the tape clutching her easel, threw him a glance and then set to work, surprised at how much the excitement of the last twenty-four hours had improved her style. At a quarter past eleven, Mrs Clutton Brock, parasol in hand, sauntered round the rocks, stepped up on to the terrace, paused when she saw the others but then came on and took her place on the bench. Theodora striding from her meeting with Mrs Turk and clasping a copy of Mowinkel on the Psalms took them all in but stayed in spite of the press. The well was, after all, a good deal quieter than the retreat house. She made herself comfortable on the terrace below the deer plaque.

Angus arrived at twelve. He glanced round the pool, located Canon Beagle and stood beside him. The old man was snoring. Theodora watched the vignette. Angus seemed to be torn between wanting to wake the Canon up and thinking that that would be unkind. He looked at his watch, caught Theodora's eye, hesitated and then came over to her.

'They've taken Bough in for questioning,' he said.

'I heard. Would he be capable of so terrible an act?'

'I suppose we're all capable given enough pressure.'

'What would that amount to in Bough's case?'

Angus shrugged. 'The police theory is that Ruth was wanting to keep his child and he was not. I cannot myself think they are right. If everyone left them alone, my impression was they might have married in a wee while.' Angus's Scottish accent, Theodora noticed, had strengthened as his emotion increased. Perhaps the effort of broaching more intimate matters, speaking openly when it was his pastoral habit to suggest or imply, imposed a strain on Angus which showed itself in his retreat to his native tongue.

'So you don't think he killed her?'

'He can be a mite uncouth on occasion but I doubt he's mad or that he'd kill someone he loved.'

'So who did, and why?'

Angus looked consideringly at her. 'Women are a great trial to the Church.'

Theodora was startled. This was a new and unlooked-for aspect of the case. What was Angus driving at? 'Ruth wasn't a professional member of the Church, only a layman. How could that affront anyone?'

Angus hesitated and then he said 'There's a long, ignoble tradition in the western Church of making women either whores or saints with nothing in between. Both Ruth and, I suppose, her mother were technically the first but in their actions, the quality of their lives, their very great kindness, they came near to the second. So men found it difficult to know how to treat them. Father Bellaire now, never felt entirely at home with them. It was a great change when Canon Tussock took over.'

Theodora failed to see where this was leading. 'Isn't that just history? Why should such attitudes have anything to do with a murder now?'

Angus sighed. 'Tradition's a grand thing. It keeps us all upright and performing, gives us a measure to measure ourselves by, if you understand me. But if you look into our Lord's own words, He Himself wasn't a deal keen on it, if you ken the gospel.'

'And Bellaire represented tradition, Tussock change?' If Angus wanted to chat about ancient history, she wouldn't stop him. 'How come Bellaire let Tussock in in the first place?'

'They were broke. Not a bawbee. Bellaire'd built the chapel and laid out the holy well with his own money. He was in hock to a rare penny. There were creditors asking.' Angus's tone well conveyed his Scottish lowland horror at the notion of importunate creditors.

'When did Tussock take over?'

'Sixty-two.'

'And the changes?'

'Oh immeasurable.'

Theodora could not detect whether he approved of them or not.

'We had mixed groups and many more of them – and merrier. I myself benefited. I first came here in Bellaire's time as a lad in my teens. Then a decade later when I was training for a teacher, I came back. It was an entirely different feel. Tusk spanned ages, sexes, classes. He was good at including. He actually liked people. It wasn't false at all. There was a lot of *bonhomie*.'

'And Bellaire?'

'Felt left out when Tussock's groups were here, threatened almost. He kept his little fellowship of laddies but they looked in at different, separate times.' Angus glanced up at Theodora. 'His focus of attention was different from Tussock's. Less on people, more, if you like to put it this way, more on God or the mystery of God, the sacramental, the seeing of God in nature. The pool, the celebration of the mass, even the beauty of the countryside around.'

'The deer-hounds.' Theodora grinned. She perfectly understood the tension Angus was trying to pin down. The Church needed both but each party tended to deride the other.

'Aye, the deer-hounds too.'

'I don't see how all that leads to this.' Theodora spread her hands to encompass the murder.'

'They both, both Bellaire and Tussock, left their residue, their spiritual successors, the consequences of which we have to deal with. Can you not sense it even with our present little group?'

'How many of them have been here before in Bellaire's time or Tussock's? Theodora was suddenly alert.

'I think all except yourself and Mrs Lemming?'

'Guy?'

'I do not think he had made a formal visit. And yet . . . it was reported in the village he came here a wee while ago. Reconnoitring maybe. He has friends amongst the travellers, I believe.'

'Angus, would Bellaire have kept any records of the pilgrims or the groups which visited here, do you suppose?'

'I have often wondered, Miss Braithwaite, but I have never put my hand on anything of the kind. Father Augustine was not that way inclined. Indeed his monetary troubles stemmed from his lack of orderliness in such matters.' Angus was stern.

'So the only way of finding out who was here at a

given time, say 1962, would be to find someone who was and get them to remember as much as possible?'

'Aye.'

'Were you here in '62, Angus?'

'I very much regret I was not.'

The forest which covered the hills round the valley of St Sylvan's had always been there. Horse chestnuts had come with the Romans and taken over from the older oak. Some English sycamore and a little pine had seeped in over the centuries. The descendants of the deer that St Sylvan had hunted remained still. The cycle of the day had not changed. The social hours were dawn and dusk, when voles and small mammals ventured out and slithered cannily through the undergrowth, foxes trotted through their territories, owls spent long minutes in concentration and then swooped. Only kestrels hunted hopefully by daylight.

Guy, aware of his predators, felt safe as houses under the canopy of summer growth in the late evening. He decided against pitching his visible orange tent and chose instead to wrap himself in his sleeping bag. He had chained his bike to a tree, checked his compass and watch and laid his plans. His friends would help him and hide him and they could only be a day or two away now. They would all come for the festival, they would all be together. Guy felt that an army was gathering to help him. The pagans, like the ungodly, the free and unrestrained would prevail and he would be in their ranks.

The only thing was, to prove his point he really ought

to get someone to get hold of the will or at least to know what was in it. Whom could he trust? 'Who will go for me?' he shouted into the trees. His final thought before pushing his head into the warm bracken was, I'll phone her tomorrow.

CHAPTER NINE

Rural Retreats

Everyone had made an effort to keep Tuesday, the day following Bough's being taken in for questioning, normal. They had all, or all except Guy, turned up punctually at the eight o'clock Eucharist. Angus had celebrated, Canon Beagle read the New Testament lesson, Theodora served. Guy's absence was felt, Ruth and Tom were remembered in prayer. Mr Clutton Brock coughed and hawked his way through the responses, Mrs Clutton Brock's eyes rarely lowered themselves from the ceiling. Mrs Lemming found herself in good voice for the hymn. At the end Angus stood on the chancel steps to say his few words.

'The events of the last few days may have made us feel that we are in danger, that we live in dangerous times just as St Sylvan did. Our temptation may be to put those events away from us, to tell ourselves that they are no more than an untypical episode which disrupts our time here. In doing that we may bring ourselves some relief. A false relief. For if we suppose there is such a thing as normal life which does not include violence, then we deceive ourselves and the truth is not in us. Death, violence, illicit passion, every deadly sin are the very stuff of normal life, there is no other, and we are not exceptions to it. For if we look into our own hearts, shall we not find those passions there? Our life's work, our pilgrimage is to grapple with such things, not to ignore, evade or secrete them, but to bring them to the full light of day, each supporting the other as best he may in that noble task.'

In the absence of Ruth, it had fallen to Theodora to prepare breakfast. No one had thought of making alternative domestic arrangements. Angus, having pronounced his grace for the fruits of the earth and work of human hands, had looked with some embarrassment towards Theodora and assured her he'd try to find someone from the village to take over the cooking. Whereupon the spirit of Anglican womanhood, that backbone of parish life, had risen to the surface and both Mrs Clutton Brock and Mrs Lemming had hurried to offer their help with lunch.

Mrs Clutton Brock settled herself at one end of the kitchen table and began shelling peas with immense dexterity, her long musician's fingers working at twice the rate of the unskilled. Mrs Lemming swerved towards the sink full of washing-up.

'We must all pull together in adversity, as Angus so

truly said, or we shan't get any lunch,' Mrs Lemming opined, flinging Fairy Liquid about with apparent enjoyment.

Theodora, who had had experience of more than one cook in a kitchen and knew it to be a recipe for disaster, was rather taken aback by her optimism.

'I've decided to stay, after all,' Mrs Lemming went on, 'so I shall need to make the best of things. At all events it's better than Tunbridge Wells and Norman.'

'I'd no idea you were thinking of leaving,' Mrs Clutton Brock looked across at her.

'Well, it's not quite what one thinks of as a retreat, this, is it? Not with violence and sudden death.'

Theodora marvelled, as she often did, at the selective hearing of those who listened to sermons. Had she not heard what Angus had said?

'I've always thought of a retreat as normal life slowed down to a pace that one could get a grip on it,' said Mrs Clutton Brock, 'like the slow movement or an andante.'

'Whereas, in fact, everything has hotted up considerably,' Mrs Lemming continued, rinsing and stacking at full steam.

Theodora didn't know whether she was glad Mrs Lemming had cheered up and was enjoying herself or whether she felt there was a degree of impropriety in her buoyancy in the face of a still unresolved murder.

'And then, of course, there are the sideshows of the skull and Father Bellaire's walking cope,' Mrs Lemming pressed on shamelessly. 'It's as though someone were trying to communicate in symbols, isn't it?' she went on, suddenly acute. 'Don't you think?' She dried her hands and turned to her two companions.

'What is being communicated?' Theodora enquired.

'I'd say the skull with the nail in it comes from someone who didn't care for Augustine Bellaire, wouldn't you? I mean it would hardly count as a friendly token.'

' "Your grisley token, my mind had broken, from worldly lust",' Mrs Clutton Brock quoted.

'How well you put things,' said Mrs Lemming with genuine admiration.

'But he's been dead seven years,' Theodora objected.

'Hatreds go on though, don't they?' Mrs Clutton Brock said. 'And accumulate and fester.' She finished her peas and turned to Theodora. 'Can I make bread?' she asked. 'If we're all staying, we shall run out tomorrow and it'll need to prove overnight to be any good.'

Theodora didn't know whether she was more surprised that Mrs Clutton Brock should ask her advice or that she should know how to make bread.

'Wholemeal in the bin, strong plain in the sack,' she answered. 'I saw yeast in the larder to your left.'

So they worked together, produced food which was more than edible and at one o'clock gathered to consume it.

The oddity of the meal was the presence of Inspector Bottomley. Early in the morning the Inspector had returned to clear up the library and marshal the remains of her incident room. She had been closeted with Angus for half an hour and then at his invitation appeared at luncheon. The sense of a mission accomplished and that being a relief was not prominent. She took little part in the conversation. While being perfectly civil, she had a watchful air as though trying to crack a secret, though whether this was to do with the crime or whether it was an attempt to fathom the religious life, Theodora could not decide. No one attempted to draw her into conversation which was, in any case, spasmodic.

When the telephone rang the entire table jumped. Inspector Bottomley reached down beside her chair into her immense briefcase, took out her mobile phone and clamped it without embarrassment to her ear. After a moment she handed it to Theodora. 'For you. A man's voice. Strong Welsh accent. Won't give a name.'

Theodora, who had a highly developed sense of etiquette, was momentarily at a loss. What *were* the conventions, governing mobile phones, *other people's* mobile phones? By her code phone calls were best received in some privacy. She looked round the table and saw a circle of expectant faces. 'If you'll excuse me,' she murmured and, clasping the novel instrument, marched from the room.

Guy's voice was unmistakable. 'Theo,' he said, 'I haven't long. Can you check the will for me and then tell the rest, or at least Angus?'

'The will?'

'My grandad's. Whoever killed Ruth has me next in mind, so you'll have to get your skates on.'

'Guy, the police have got Ruth's killer. They think Tom Bough was responsible.'

'Who?'

'Bough.'

'The silly beggars. That nail in the skull. It meant what it said. Death to those who oppose Bellaire, if I'm not mistaken. And Father Augustine was not my grandad's friend.'

'Guy, there's another possible interpretation.'

'No there isn't. Look, my grandad's solicitors are in Harrogate, Broadbent and Helliwell. Senior partner died just before grandad, but someone must be dealing with it. Get in touch, could you? Verify the details of the *last* – got that? – the *last* will. Can't be more than eighteen months old. Grandad told me. Believe me, I know what I'm saying.'

'Guy, come back. Come and deal with it yourself, tell the police what you know.'

'Nope. I'm going to keep out of the way until they've got it sorted.'

'Where are you?'

The line had gone dead. Theodora stood for a moment in the corridor not knowing which way to turn. Finally she went back into the dining-room. Six pairs of eyes looked expectant.

'Guy,' she said as nonchalantly as possible. 'Just phoning to say he's well. We're not to worry about him.' She looked at Inspector Bottomley.

The latter was not pleased. 'You might have passed him across,' she said bitterly. 'The little tyke. I need his statement, as well he must know. Where is he?'

Theodora was apologetic. 'I'm afraid he didn't say.'

'Can't you trace the call?' Mrs Lemming asked. She'd read detective novels in which this was regularly and easily done.

'Not with a mobile unless we know they're coming and not always then. The only certain thing we can say is that it can't be more than twenty miles away because it wouldn't come through if it were. I dare say we'll pick him up soon enough. I've got a call out for him and the travellers' van.'

Angus cleared his throat. 'I don't know if you have any particular van in mind, Inspector, but at this time of year there tend to be a number of travellers coming down to the well. They come to the St Sylvan's Day celebrations which fall this year on this coming Friday.'

'If need be we'll question the lot,' said Inspector Bottomley grimly. 'I don't mind telling you, Mr Bootle, as I said this morning, there are aspects of this case with which I am far from happy.'

Mr Clutton Brock leaned forward and looked Inspector Bottomley in the face. 'I suppose all you liberal women are the same, soft on crimes of passion.'

'I am not a liberal woman, Mr Clutton Brock, if you mean anything by that phrase. I am a police inspector and I like nice tidy cases with all the evidence laid out so that the Crown Prosecution Service can't make a pig's ear of it. We all want justice, I imagine?' She glared round the table. 'Well then. Justice depends on having got at the truth.' With that she reached down for her bag and departed.

Angus felt grace was called for and several of the older pilgrims realised an urge for an afternoon nap.

Theodora, stretched out under the mulberry tree in the garden, reflected on the place, time and problems which confronted her. She allowed her eye to wander round the space. The espaliered apple and pear trees cast a net over the stone wall. Their shadows were starting to creep over the beds towards the lawn. The mulberry's fruit was beginning to fall in the final heat of summer. Away by the back door she could make out the earthenware pots of herbs. Ruth had known and loved, planted and cherished the garden. A virgin in a garden – an image of a complete world. A tree the leaves of which drop to form its own self-sustaining compost, another such. The kitchen was a domain, a serene and ordered kingdom, and beyond it lay the round pool, a cosmic centre in which Ruth had perished. We are made by places, we cannot remain indifferent to them, Theodora thought. The Church knows that, or used to. Certainly Bellaire had known it, that was his genius, his contribution to the Kingdom. Tussock recognised it and jumped in to populate it, to spread its benefits more widely. But in the course of that had come some flaw, some fault or fall in the Eden.

It was almost as though in killing Ruth someone had wanted to destroy the principle of the place. What could go wrong in such a paradise? Was it the people who came here? She let her mind wander over the relationships of the present group in so far as they were known to her. Ruth and Bough, she was certain, were at ease with one another. She had seen them with her own eyes. Surely one can't be so deceived in such matters? Even if they were not bound by the sacrament of marriage and their ages were disparate, she would swear they were content.

Canon Beagle, too, seemed sane enough. He strove to be fair, to endure and to be resourceful in the face of what, for an athlete, would be great adversity. His religious observance was disciplined, heroically unfashionable and it seemed to sustain him. What about Angus? He had a young Scottish wife back at his vicarage and two children and a dog. He was scrupulous to the point of ridicule but he wasn't tense or rigid with the effort. He meditated on Scripture and the great doctrinal truths and evidently they nurtured him. And Guy, what of him? He was undoubtedly odd. His physical suddenness, his elusive retreats if matters got too much for him and his flashes of acuteness mixed with a naivety which made Theodora feel old, were they symptoms of some deeper disturbance? Was he perhaps schizophrenic? Or had he had too much religion forced upon him too early and suffered, in consequence, a reaction? He had, nevertheless, evolved his techniques which, though they might not be orthodoxly religious techniques, seemed to suit him, a sort of joyful deviousness which might not be quite sane.

Even Mrs Lemming, though shackled, as she felt herself to be, to Norman, had her methods. She liked a hymn. She had her sketching. And what about the Clutton Brocks? Theodora remembered them sitting on the sofa in the library when they first came. They hardly engaged with each other. He took refuge in his hay fever, tense and obsessed – by what? She fended off the world with a cultivated coldness which forbade sympathy as an intrusion. She had the air of hearing distant music. But, taken altogether, they seemed such an ordinary collection of people. How could any of them be killers? And, if so, where could the destructive force come from? Theodora wondered sleepily.

Keep to the concrete, she told herself, rousing herself. Keep to the skull. Was Mrs Lemming on to something when she said it looked like a way of communicating in symbols? And which way could those symbols be taken? It all depended on the nail, Theodora felt. It could be taken as a warning that Bellaire's reign was flawed. On the other hand it could be understood, as Guy had it, that a death was presaged. And then there was the cope. Why should anyone, as it were, make the cope walk? And if all three events were connected, did that imply that the key to the mystery lay in the past history of the place? Perhaps if she could find out more about who had stayed there and when and perhaps, too, if she followed up Guy's request to verify the conditions of the will, there might be a way forward.

Theodora was aware that a horn had sounded twice outside the front of the guest-house. Ever prone to take on responsibilities, she raised herself on one elbow and listened. The horn sounded again. She rose and made her way out of the garden towards the front of the house.

'You see, Miss Braithwaite,' said Martha Broad as she clasped and unclasped her large hands over the steering wheel of the old Humber, 'I feel I have a pastoral duty to Mr Bough, I mean Tom's father. I really ought to try to see him. Angus asked me to. He can't go because the Bishop wants to see him this afternoon. I gather it's about the closure of the centre.'

They were parked in the drive outside the guest-house. The chapel clock had struck three. The only thing I want right now Theodora thought, is a telephone, preferably of the fixed variety. Would an afternoon with Miss Broad put her in the way of such a thing?

'I could offer you tea after the trip, if that's any induce-ment. My father, I'm afraid, is in London at the moment but the house is very pleasant in this weather.'

This was not what Theodora had wanted from a retreat. It really was too much like parish life; visits, engagements, duties.

'Of course I'll come, if you feel I could be of any help,' she answered.

Miss Broad swivelled her sweet smile towards Theo-dora, engaged a gear and fought with the handbrake.

'Mr Bough isn't the easiest person in the world to visit. I don't know how he'll take his son's being questioned by the police.'

Miss Broad had set off at a fair pace over ground clearly familiar to her. Hedges and stone walls hurtled past. The car predated seat belts and Miss Broad had not thought to add them. Theodora held on to her seat and listened to the springs pinging beneath her.

'I always thought Ruth and Tom were genuinely fond of each other. And, of course, it was time for Ruth to settle down, and Tom too.'

'Miss Broad, two days before Ruth was killed she told her aunt, Mrs Turk, that she expected relations of her father's to be amongst our party of pilgrims. Would you know who that might be?'

Miss Broad looked unhappy. 'It's a long time ago. I was only twenty or so when Naomi Swallow was at St Sylvan's.'

'Were you there in her last year before she had Ruth, 1962 or thereabouts?'

'Yes, it was '62. We were all there that year for the St Sylvan's festival. It was the year the new chapel windows were dedicated. Lavinia Strong was there and her fiancé, Victor Clutton Brock. The tension between Bellaire and Tussock was at its height. Lavinia was just beginning to make her name. I remember thinking that Victor was feeling his nose out of joint. It must be hard on a man, I mean a nonentity, to be married to a talented woman.'

The thought seemed to inspire Miss Broad. She pressed harder on the accelerator and though the speed did not discernibly increase, the noise did.

'They manage it less well, you feel, than the other way round?' Theodora shouted above the cacophony.

'Well, it's more usual the other way round, so I expect we have more practice.'

'How did Tussock and Bellaire actually get on?' Theodora enquired.

'Look,' said Miss Broad, applying the brakes. 'Famous view.'

She swerved on to an outcrop of rock and drew up. She waved her hand in the general direction of the valley and the wooded hillside beyond. 'Still all Broad land, except St Sylvan's. Grandfather gave it to Bellaire. Not a prudent move given the Church's financial incompetence. We should have had a reverter put on it. Still, no point in repining. Though I must say I shudder at a heritage centre. The vulgarity of that appalling man Peake.'

She turned back to Theodora's original question. 'Bellaire and Tussock.' She revved up and raced on before continuing. 'I expect you can imagine. Bellaire was in the Catholic tradition, Tussock the evangelical. As far as the running of the centre was concerned, Bellaire's was the monastic model, Tusk was more the boy scout, getting-people-together one. Both had a point, both were good at it in their different ways. Both rather excluded. If you weren't matey, you'd be left out of Tusk's lot. If you weren't a man, you'd probably be uncomfortable with Bellaire's party.'

Miss Broad ground her gears to increase the pace of the car to cope with the track which had replaced the road.

'How did they come together in the first place to share the centre?'

'Tusk was ever a man with an eye to the main chance and Bellaire was broke. Tusk's money came from his wife. They were in worsted originally, later beer. Plenty there. I think Bellaire thought that because he was better bred and better educated than Tusk he'd be able to manage him.' Miss Broad snorted at such naivety.

'And he couldn't?'

'No way. Tusk played it very carefully at first. The place was supposed to be run by a board of trustees set up by Bellaire originally. Usual Church way of doing things, get a few old pals together, never mind whether they had any relevant experience for running anything. It was all very hierarchical. Bellaire was called Senior Warden of the shrine, the others were Brother Wardens. Fancy vestments. The lot. But there was some sort of coup when Tussock put money in. It came to a head that summer.'

'How so?'

The road had by this time given out entirely. They were travelling over a deeply rutted grass track against the raised bits of which the Humber's exhaust could be heard scraping. In between these distressing noises, Theodora heard Miss Broad say, 'I never knew the details. I only saw the results. But Henry Beagle knew something. He was of Bellaire's band, of course. I had the feeling Tussock had a hold over Bellaire from then on. Lot of the older brother wardens went and some new ones came in, slab-faced archdeacon types who could read a balance sheet, if nothing else.'

'Henry Beagle was there in the summer of '62?'

'Oh yes. He *was* a handsome man thirty years ago. Rising fifty then, of course but *such* a noble profile.'

'Was Mrs Lemming there?'

'Who? No. I don't think so. She's a tiresome little woman.'

'She has her problems.'

Miss Broad was not interested in Mrs Lemming's problems.

'Who else was there who is still about now?'

'I don't remember any... oh yes, of course, Tom Bough's father, Bob Bough was there. I remember at the party after the Eucharist, he'd been brought in to help with the drinks. He was so spry then and he finds it so difficult to get about now.'

'So the men present at the '62 festival were, at least, Bough senior, Bellaire, Tussock, Beagle, Clutton Brock. Any more?'

'There was a bishop, a fair number of congregation but no one else resident, I think.' Miss Broad didn't seem to see what Theodora was getting at. 'Look,' she said, descending down a couple of painful gears, 'we're nearly there.'

Theodora looked round. The track had turned into a clearing. Old milk crates, half-buried in cow parsley, and buckets without bottoms loomed up. A couple of tractor tyres of immense size were tethered for some arcane purpose to trees. At the far end of the clearing Theodora saw a pile of chopped logs stacked to a height of about seven feet. A wisp of smoke curled into the air above it and following it down Theodora detected first a tin chimney, then an aperture which might have been a window, then a door. Bob Bough's cabin. A line of socks, no one of which related to any other, proclaimed a bachelor's or presumably, a widower's establishment. To the left a row of potatoes flowered, to the right a coop of chickens clucked their appreciative welcome to the visitors. Mr Bough believed in being self-supporting.

'The Boughs were always woodland folk,' said Miss Broad with no trace of whimsy. She brought a powerful elbow to bear on the middle of the steering wheel and Theodora jumped as the noise of the horn echoed round the clearing.

'Bob doesn't care to be taken by surprise and he's very deaf now.'

They got out and the door slammed in the silence left after the noise of the horn. They paused for a moment as though in homage to the surprising spirit of the place. Then Miss Broad strode forward towards the pile of wood. Miss Broad's knock was answered by a volley of barks. The door was opened a couple of inches and a shrivelled old man gazed up at the two tall women.

'I'm warning you lot. I moithered with bloody bobbies.'

'Not police, Bob, just me and a friend of mine. I've brought a bit of parkin.' Miss Broad proffered her lure.

The door opened with surprising swiftness. Mr Bough put a skinny hand on Miss Broad and took the gift with a quick furtive movement as though if he took it in that way he might not need to return gratitude. He wore a grey flannel shirt of the same ancestry as his son's and a pair of black trousers ending in large heavy boots.

'Come in, lass. Shut up yer silly beggar,' he roared with sudden power over his shoulder to the dog.

Mr Bough's cabin was as idiosyncratic within as without. Theodora edged round the door which Mr Bough mercifully left open. A smell of wood-smoke, dog and varnish wafted out. There was a stone floor and an armchair with a carpet thrown over it. On the table was a jumble of washing-up at one end and the tools of woodcarving at the other. Tied to one of the table legs was an old evil-eyed collie, still rumbling with growls. As she grew accustomed to the darkness, Theodora became aware that every inch of wall space was covered with wooden musical instruments: flutes, oboes, recorders, parts of fiddles and cellos, and parts to which Theodora could not put a name.

'I've just brewed up,' said Mr Bough hospitably. He produced a pair of enormous cups, one of which had a handle and pushed them across the table in their direction.

'We just happened to be passing,' Miss Broad shouted in Bob's direction. It sounded even more unlikely turned up forte than it would have done at normal volume.

'Oh, aye. They've been here twice,' Mr Bough chuntered on. 'I told them. I said I know nowt about it. Tom's his own master and has been since our Dolly passed on. Forty-three year going on Pancake Tuesday. They didn't take a blind bit of notice. Might as well spit out for all the good it does.' Mr Bough's small bloodshot eyes swelled and watered with the injustice of it all.

'Tom hasn't been charged, Bob. They just want to ask him a few questions.'

'You play a bit, eh?,' Bob's question was addressed to Theodora who had been gazing at the wall display. Conversing with Miss Broad seemed to interest him less.

'No, only listen.'

'If Tom is charged, Bob,' Miss Broad knew her pastoral duty and persevered with it even in the face of discouragement, 'I'll take you down to visit him in Wormald, if you want.'

169

Bob had the only saucer. He blew a small tidal wave of tea towards them, with fine judgement desisted just before it slopped over, allowed a moment for it to subside and then sucked it through his teeth.

'Bloody bobbies. Bloody clergy. He'd never have killed Ruth Swallow, wouldn't our Tom. He's not a bad lad when all's said and done.'

'Who might have killed her, Mr Bough?' Theodora asked quietly.

'They're not all they're cracked up to be down there. Woe to them that devise iniquity.' He turned towards Theodora as though she might be in need of an explanation of his reference. 'Micah two, one,' he said smugly. 'Used to be in St Sylvan's at Rest choir when I was a little lad.' He turned to Miss Broad with venom. 'Before I knew better.'

'What iniquity?' Theodora asked.

A look of cunning came over Mr Bough's face. He dropped a tone or two and said, 'Bellaire, he was a wrong 'un. A right nasty piece of work with them young lads.'

Miss Broad rose hastily from her seat. 'Well, Bob, think on what I've said. If it comes to stick and lift, I'll get you down to Wormald to see Tom. Don't you worry. But we must all hope and pray that it doesn't come to that. I think we should be going now,' she said rapidly to Theodora, 'and leave Mr Bough in peace.'

As they lurched back down the cart-track, Theodora said, 'Would he be right, do you suppose, about Bellaire?'

'It was all a long time ago,' answered Miss Broad.

CHAPTER TEN

Holy Vestments

'Hello,' said Theodora. 'Aunt Jane? Theodora here.'

A clipped voice at the other end of the phone said, 'Just a minute please. I have a builder at the door.'

Theodora clasped the phone of the village phone box at St Sylvan's at Rest and counted the change available to her. She trusted it would be enough.

'Hello,' the voice resumed. 'Who is that?'

'Theodora.'

'Oh, my dear, how very nice. Hugh said you'd ring. Where are you?'

'St Sylvan's at Rest, the retreat house.'

'Really? Are you going to come over for a meal. I'm free, where are we, Friday, this Friday. Say seven o'clock?'

'I'm on retreat, Aunt. I really can't get away.'

'I thought they'd broken all that up. Some sort of

murder. I read it in the *Yorkshire Post*.'

'Yes, there has been a murder but it hasn't stopped the retreat.'

'I see. So you won't be coming to see me after all.' The tone was miffed.

'I'd love to but we don't finish here till Saturday morning. I thought perhaps . . . I wondered if I could stop over with you Saturday night.'

'Saturday. Well I don't know.'

'Not if it's inconvenient.'

'No, no. Not at all.' The voice made a moral effort and recovered humour and real kindness. 'I'd be delighted to see you. Come as early as you can. Now I really must . . .'

'Aunt, there is just one thing. I wondered if I could possibly ask you a favour?'

'Well?' The tone modulated to suspicion.

'I need some information from Broadbent and Helliwell, the solicitors.'

'We don't use them. I always go to Clegg and Rambottom up Leeds road.'

'No. I don't want to use them professionally. Look it's all a bit difficult.'

'Well, couldn't it wait until I see you? I've got the builders in and if I don't give them tea every two hours they stop and go off to another job. I'm in competition with Reg Crowther who, I believe, cheats by giving them doughnuts.'

'Aunt, look, I really am awfully sorry but I do need this help, this information.' Theodora fumbled for more change and rammed an unwilling fifty-pence piece into the aperture. 'A man's freedom may depend on it.'

Really she thought, I'm being melodramatic. How do I know that? 'I've been ringing Broadbent and Helliwell all day, well twice, and I can't get through to anyone senior enough to deal with what I want and St Sylvan's isn't on the phone, so I have to keep making a special trek down to the village and I really can't keep on like this.' Theodora was aware she sounded desperate, which she was.

'What do you want?' Miss Rathbone's tone suggested she scented a challenge. She was good at challenges, getting information out of recalcitrant sources was a speciality of hers. She'd spent twenty years running hospitals in the colonies, before returning to Harrogate to sit on the bench, various school governing bodies, the parish council, anything, really, which one could sit on. A managing woman, Hugh called her with distaste, though he acknowledged her worth.

'I need to know the contents of Canon Ben Tussock's last, it must be his *last*, will.'

'Poor Ben. I knew him for over thirty years. I know some people found him bogus but he could be great fun.'

'Yes. Yes, I'm sure he could. The point is, though, I need to know about the terms of his will, his *last* . . .'

'Why?'

'The contents ought to concern the disposition of money and property with regard to the foundation of St Sylvan's as against his relations,' said Theodora carefully. 'I gather there were at least two wills, an early one which, I think, the Church authorities are working on and a later one. It may provide a motive for murder . . .'

'Leave it with me,' said the voice authoritatively. 'I know Gerald Broadbent quite well. We sit on the same parish council. Now, I really must go. I can see my builder sitting in his van. Don't worry, love. I'll get back to you.'

Theodora put down the phone and heard the last of her change clank through the system. She felt a surge of relief before it occurred to her to wonder how her godmother would do that, given the lack of telephone communication with St Sylvan's.

Canon Beagle shut the door of the vestry behind him and carefully manoeuvred his chair into place beside the press. The vestry was rather larger than one might have supposed, he reflected. Didn't like to be cramped when he was vesting, didn't Augustine. Give the deer-hounds room. Canon Beagle glanced at his watch. Half an hour to supper and no one likely to disturb him. He'd checked on all of them. Bootle (pity the chap hadn't kept his noon appointment with him, he looked reliable but you could never tell these days) was still with the Bishop. The Clutton Brock female was practising in her room. Theodora had just got back from the village and gone into the kitchen. Victor Clutton Brock had strode off towards the village. Very unfit man. Mrs Lemming was up at the pool sketching away as though her life depended on it.

It was a long time since he'd been in here, he reflected.

The light from the single roundel picked out the brass cross on top of the press. On the wall were a couple of photographs. One showed the old farmhouse before it had been extended by the guest-house. Must have been taken just before the war. Very pleasant it looked too. Pity people had to improve things. The other photograph showed a group of people strung out, looking rather conscious, as people asked to pose do. At one end was Tussock with his famous smile dressed for summer in a linen suit but with a clerical collar. At the other end was Bellaire in a soutane, every stiff button visible. He must have spent a fortune on dress, poor fellow.

In between were ranged a number of others. Canon Beagle adjusted his glasses and peered closer. 'Yes, there we all were,' he murmured. He gazed at his middle-aged self. I must have been about fifty. He looked into his confident and, as men would say (and women too, he admitted), handsome features. He passed a hand over his face and felt his tongue round his teeth. Decayed a bit since then. Though still pretty fit and fighting, he told himself. In the photograph his hand rested on the chair of a seated figure, a woman. Who would that be? Lavinia Strong, of course. Pretty she'd been then and smiling, almost with confidence, towards the camera. Life, or anyway life with Victor, had pushed her inwards, Canon Beagle thought. And next to her was Victor, little Victor with a good growth of fair floppy hair. Lost a lot of that. Beside him was another woman. Ruth, no, not Ruth of course, her mother Naomi Swallow. Handsomer than her daughter but a clear resemblance. Then a couple of men very young and fresh and innocent, just as Augustine liked them. Finally, he could make out in the background the unsmiling face of a servant who looked familiar too. Then it came to him. Bough. Tom Bough. No, Bob Bough, it must be, the father. Underneath the photograph were printed the words: Dedication of Chapel Windows, St Sylvan's Day, 25 July 1962.

Canon Beagle sat back in his chair. That was the last time he'd been here. It seemed like yesterday. What had he done with his life in between? The clock in the tower struck the quarter. He shook himself. Better get cracking. But still he hesitated. One half of him had waited thirty years to be sure. The other half felt he did not at any price want to know. He reminded himself why he had come, why he had made this immense physical and emotional effort, made, in fact, a pilgrimage, if not to set at rest an old misery, to die knowing rather than in ignorance, even if knowledge were painful. Then, of course, there would be the pleasure of discovering if he were right, both about the hiding-place and about the stratagems, the dealings moral and ecclesiastical which had orchestrated events.

He surveyed the press. It had three drawers. He eased the first open. The shallowest of the three, it contained a box of matches, three candles, a packet of communion wafers and a tube of cough lozenges. He slammed it shut and tried the second. A clean surplice and a red stole of the season. Must be Angus's. How about the last one? Bit like a fairytale, the third choice is the important one. He moved his chair back a little to give himself more space. His hips were aching and he felt the sweat gathering on his brow. It was the deepest of the drawers. Carefully he balanced its weight on the handles and pulled. It stuck fast. Hell's teeth, surely it wasn't locked? He looked carefully at the wood. No sign of a lock. He relaxed his shoulders and wrists and gently tried again. It slid out sweetly.

There, lying neat and compact, close to view was the cope, red and green, white and gold. Green chestnut-leaf foliage with red fruit wound from collar to hem and, yes, just as he had remembered them, two deer-hounds extravagantly elongated, embroidered in white silk, leaped at – what were they leaping at? Gently he turned the folds over and saw they were leaping towards the golden head of an antlered deer which, when the garment was worn, must have been displayed full across the back. Canon Beagle sucked his teeth. Some ingenuity would be needed to get Christian symbolism out of that lot. Still, it was a fine design, wonderfully executed – 'To the glory of God, let us hope,' Canon Beagle murmured.

It brought back that festal Eucharist of thirty years ago more vividly than anything else could. That was when the fight between Tussock and Bellaire had come to a head. He couldn't have been paying much attention to things or else he would have remembered the design. But then he'd had a lot on his mind and the main focus of everyone's attention had been the windows. He'd never been back. First there'd been China, then Tussock had really taken over and there'd been less point, what with one thing and another. Would he have the courage for the next step? Come on, Henry, he exhorted himself, in the tones of his grandfather who had been a missionary bishop in Africa when they still had cannibals, faintheartedness has never been your way. He leaned forward and drew the cope from its place. It was heavy, heavier than he had ever worn; all that gold thread. He noticed some repair-work had been carefully and skilfully done to the collar. Now where would the old devil have . . .? With a quick movement he threw the collar and the upper part of the cope over the top of the press and edged his chair foward, shutting the drawer with his legs. Then swiftly he felt along the line of the shoulders. They were slightly padded. He turned them inside out. The lining was of white silk which stopped just below the shoulder line and was continued with stiff cotton. He slipped his thumb up under the seam and, lo and behold, there was a pocket and on the other side, a matching one. Damn his hands for being so swollen, the joints arthritic. He fumbled first with the right side and then with the left. Carefully he edged out the packages of papers which had laid in each since 1962.

'Look here,' said Inspector Bottomley to Theodora, 'are you telling me that Ben Tussock made a will leaving everything to his daughter and if she should die within a year of him, to his grandson provided he should be accepted for Anglican orders and if he isn't or if he dies within a similar time span, then everything goes to the St Sylvan's Trust for the perpetuation of the pilgrimage centre?'

'Yes,' said Theodora. She had to admit she was proud of her godmother. Miss Rathbone had rung the post office early that Wednesday morning, twenty-four hours after receiving her commission. She'd got, of course, Mrs Turk. Theodora did rather wonder what those two formidable women had said to each other. Mrs Turk had rung Angus at Rest Vicarage and Angus had waited till after breakfast to say there was a message from her godmother. Would Theodora ring her but not before eleven because she had the builders in?

Theodora had listened carefully to Miss Rathbone's information and then decided that Inspector Bottomley was the proper person to have it. She resigned herself to putting yet more money into the telephone box and felt she would pretty well own the machine before the retreat was finished. They'd arranged to meet at two p.m. beside the well. Their ideas of time coincided. At five to two each of them had pushed their way through the bushes and scrambled between the rocks to the terrace. They had elected to sit on the bench usually occupied by Mrs Clutton Brock. It was slightly shaded by the huge ilex. The perfect round circle of water lay quiet and untroubled below them. As Theodora looked out she wondered if it was from here that the stone which had ended Ruth's life and been hurled.

'Tussock made two wills. The first left everything to his wife. Pretty noble since she'd given it to him in the first place. Marriage settlements like that ought not to be allowed. Then when Muriel developed Alzheimer's he remade the will.'

'What sort of sums are we talking about?' asked the Inspector.

'Three-quarters of a million at the very least.'

'Worth killing for.'

'Exactly.'

'And the daughter?' The Inspector pressed on.

'Is named in the will as Ruth Swallow.'

'No explanations?'

'No explanations, no excuses, no mention even of the mother's name, nothing, apparently.'

'Cool customer. And him a clergyman.'

'Yes,' said Theodora bleakly. She wasn't going to discuss the sins of the flesh with an outsider.

'How would this work out as a motive for killing her?'

'Well it would rank at least as high as her carrying a child, which we have no reason to think the father did not want.'

'*Cui bono?*' asked Inspector Bottomley. She liked the phrase.

'Ruth first, then Guy, then the foundation of St Sylvan.'

'So Guy has to be a suspect. He'd benefit considerably. And that being so, I really do need to get hold of him.' Inspector Bottomley didn't like to admit that she was both surprised and worried by the police's inability to lay hands on him. The lad marched around with an orange tent and a yellow mountain bike. By all the probabilities he ought to be within a twenty-mile radius of the centre, in territory most of which was forest. It should have been a piece of cake. Still, she wasn't going to share her professional worries with an outsider.

'It's an odd condition,' she pressed on, 'Guy to be a priest before he could inherit.'

'I suppose the thinking would be family first, St Sylvan's next. And if the family were to be a priest then he might well want to carry on funding the foundation.'

'But for the foundation to be sure of benefiting, Ruth had to be dead within a twelvemonth.'

'Yes. Though, in fact, if he'd bothered to know Ruth, I think he would have found that she loved the place so much she might well have devoted any resources she inherited to keeping it going.'

'But if he didn't know her he couldn't guarantee that.'

'No, I suppose not.' Theodora felt a surge of anger at Canon Tussock. How could he not have acknowledged his own daughter during her life? How could he not have wanted to know her? To know her quality, to have an authoritative hand in forming and enhancing it, in seeing it had proper scope? What was he thinking of? His own reputation presumably.

'Who would know of the terms of the will?'

'There's no reason to suppose that Ruth did, but Guy did.'

'Haven't the lawyers been a bit slow off the mark? I mean since she was the first legatee, shouldn't they have informed her?'

'I gather from my godmother that the senior partner died a few days after Canon Tussock, so there might have been a delay. Guy, on the other hand, had made inquiries and had been told he inherited if Canon Tussock's daughter died within a twelvemonth. The solicitors say Guy assumed the old man was wandering since he knew of no daughter.'

'So his assumption would be he would get the lot.'

'Unless he didn't become a priest or . . .'

'Unless he died too before the year's end.'

'Right. And I think from that phone call I had from him he's hiding because he thinks someone who would like the money to go to the foundation has it in mind to kill him to make sure of it.'

'It's possible,' Inspector Bottomley ruminated. 'On the other hand that could just be a ploy to put us off if he had actually killed Ruth. Did Ruth never find out who her father was?'

'Mrs Turk said that Ruth *did* know. She came and saw her the night before our party arrived and told her that some of her father's relations were coming for the week.'

'How do you reckon she'd found out, if the lawyers hadn't told her?'

Theodora grinned. 'Come and see how the religious mind works.'

Together they scrambled down through the rocks and made their way to the chapel. It was light and silent. The sanctuary lamp was an unobtrusive red blob in the distance. Theodora led Inspector Bottomley down the tiny aisle and stopped at the chancel steps. The east window was of plain glass so that it let in the morning sun. The two windows to the north and south, however, were of coloured glass. Theodora pointed to the south window. It showed Christ in the Garden of Gethsemane at the moment of Judas's betrayal. The figure of Judas leaned towards Christ. One hand reached to embrace Him, the other was held behind him. In that hand was a skull. But it was the face of Judas which attracted the Inspector's attention. The face was unmistakably the face in the portrait in the hall of the guest-house, the face of Augustine Bellaire.

Inspector Bottomley gazed at it for a moment. 'I take it Tussock commissioned that one?'

'Yes. You can see the name of the donor at the bottom left-hand corner. However, if you turn round you can see Bellaire's revenge.'

Inspector Bottomley revolved to gaze at the northern light. The artist had executed a picture of an ancient male figure in a meadow of corn. He was leaning on a scythe and beside him was an egg-timer. Peering round the egg-timer was the smiling face of a ram. The face of the male figure and the face of the ram resembled each other and both bore some likeness to Ben Tussock.

'I don't get it,' said Inspector Bottomley.

'Father time, Death the Reaper, or as I think Ruth understood it, "I am the mower Damon known Through all the meadows I have mown." '

'Keep going.'

'The figure of the mower has a double significance. It could be taken as an allusion both to death and to mowing as sexual conquest.'

'And that, coupled with the ram, leaves us in no doubt as to Augustine Bellaire's notion of what Canon Tussock's habits were.'

'Right.'

'Didn't care for each other?'

'Right.'

'Bit public, quarrelling in glass.'

'Religious polemic: a particularly bitter genre.'

'When did you work this lot out?'

Theodora blushed. 'I came in here to meditate on the afternoon of the murder. I sat in the chancel. It sort of stared out at me after a bit.'

Inspector Bottomley nodded. She turned away from the windows and sat down in a pew. 'Now let's work this lot out,' she said. 'Tussock calls Augustine Bellaire a Judas. Why?'

Theodora filled her in on Bob Bough's sentiments about Father Augustine. 'Betrayal of what are usually taken to be central Christian sexual values.'

'And Bellaire calls Tussock a reaper and a ram because he knew about Ruth or rather her mother Naomi. How does this help us?'

'Either someone thought the Tussock money ought to go to the foundation or perhaps one of Bellaire's lads is doing a bit of revenge on the Tussock family. Or perhaps both of those motives combined. You do see, don't you,' Theodora leaned forward and fixed a serious eye on the Inspector, 'it opens up the whole area of motive quite considerably.'

'You don't think Tom Bough did it, then?'

'Oh, come on. If Tom wanted to kill his woman he might beat her up or throttle her in a mad hig. But he's not the sort to hang about and then heave a rock at her from a distance.'

'I see what you mean. Have you done this sort of thing before?'

'Well, I did know a dean who got his throat cut when I was doing a placement at Bow St Aelfric, and then there was a residentiary canon out at Medwich who got his neck broken quite deservedly.'

'Yes, OK, I get your point. Do you get paid for it?'

Theodora was scandalised. She let the tasteless remark lie between them for a moment and then resumed. 'What worries me is the method of killing Ruth. It has religious, well biblical, overtones. Stoning is the sort of thing which happens to people who are ritually or morally unclean. It's a way of killing without, literally without, getting your hands dirty. So as a killer you stay pure whilst dispatching the impure.'

Inspector Bottomley considered this. 'I don't know what you see in religion.'

'Well, as I said, it has other strengths. It's not all as bad as that.'

'I think that's about as bad as I've met. Such deliberate wickedness. So smug.'

'The point is, would it fit in here?'

'Would Guy be accepted for orders if he wanted to go that way?' Inspector Bottomley's mind was clearly running on the eccentricities of religion.

'I really don't know. Some very odd people do seem to be accepted nowadays.'

'I think we've got to go one step at a time. First we need Guy, then we shall see what offers. You don't know where he is, do you?' She fixed Theodora with her inquisitorial eye.

Theodora turned away. 'No,' she said. 'Not for certain at this moment.'

'Well think on. And if any ideas should come to you, we'd like to know immediately.'

'Of course.' Theodora was reassuring. 'What will you do about Tom Bough? Presumably you won't want to charge him now?'

'Have to think about that. We might keep him in a while longer. Chief Constables like to feel they've got a bird in hand.'

'Deliberate wickedness and smugness,' said Theodora tartly.

CHAPTER ELEVEN

Pilgrims' Tales

Canon Beagle wheeled his chair closer to the library table and spread the documents out. Then he turned to Theodora and said, 'I would like you to look at these and then I think we should discuss Miss Swallow's death. I'll take them in date order.'

Theodora would have preferred to be out in the morning sun. It was Wednesday already. She needed to start thinking about the catering for the festival on Friday. She wanted to try to get hold of Guy preferably before Inspector Bottomley got to him. She had wondered if she ought to visit Tom Bough if he was still in prison, or, anyway, offer to help Martha Broad to get his father down to Wormald. But whilst she was turning over the claims of rival duties, Canon Beagle had mown her down in his chair and shepherded her into the dining-room. He'd been insistent, even peremptory.

She looked over the papers. There were three. The first was on thick cream paper which even now, thirty years after its date, was only just beginning to discolour at the edges. It had a black embossed crest on it of a Roman soldier standing with drawn sword between the antlers of a deer. It was headed St Sylvan's Pilgrimage Centre. The date was 1 May 1962. The hand was bold and flowing. The ink was black and strong. It read:

My dear Tussock,

The topic on which I have to approach you is a painful one. I hope you will believe me when I say I have given it much thought and prayer before writing to you about it. It has come to my notice that, to put not too fine a point on it, you have formed an adulterous relationship with Naomi Swallow. I need hardly point out that Miss Swallow is a servant here and as such in my especial care. I need hardly point out also that you have a wife taken in accordance with the laws of the Church and have been married to her on my computation for twenty years.

I do not know what your intentions are with regard to Miss Swallow. It seems to me hardly likely that you intend to divorce Muriel and start again outside, as it needs must be, the life of the Church. Whatever you intend to do, however, will necessitate your resignation from the Board of Trustees of this Foundation of St Sylvan and your ceasing to be a Brother Warden.

I think I need not advert to the unease, I may
say, the unhappiness, which at times your contact
with this Holy Foundation has caused me and indeed
others like me. I was and shall remain grateful for
the help which you were able, through Muriel's
money, to offer the Foundation at a time when its
financial position was straitened. Happily that time
is now behind us.

I expect to receive your resignation and promise
of cessation of all further contact with us before the
end of the month. I am sure that you feel, as I do,
that your appearance at this year's Festival of St
Sylvan would, in the circumstances, be inappropriate.

On a happier matter, I enclose the final account
for your settlement for the new chapel windows. The
designs remain to be finalised and I expect those
decisions now to be left in my hands.

In conclusion, if I do not receive your resignation
within my stipulated time, I shall have no alternative
but to draw the matter to the attention of the Archbishop. Believe me, in Christ,
　　Augustine Bellaire.

Theodora looked up. Left to herself she would have
laughed aloud. In Canon Beagle's presence she felt it
kinder and more politic to keep a straight face. He himself gave no indication of his feelings. His large handsome profile was turned away from her. Without looking
at her he slid the second document across the table.

This was a letter on the same sort of writing paper as

189

the first. Since it was undated and there were some small crossings-out, Theodora understood it to be draft. It read:

> Your Grace,
>   It is with the greatest reluctance that I have to draw your attention to the misconduct of the gravest kind of one of your priests, your Missioner at Large, the Revd Benjamin Tussock. I have recently had evidence given me of this priest's adultery with one of the female servants of this foundation. There can, I fear, be no mistake in the case as the girl has herself confessed to me that she is expecting his child as a result of his attentions.
>   I make no judgements, noting only my great distress that the Holy Spring of St Sylvan should be polluted by any act of this kind.
>   I am Your Grace's most obedient. . . .

The letter was unsigned but the provenance obvious. How very much Augustine had enjoyed writing it, Theodora thought. Had he sent it or not?

'Next,' said Canon Beagle poker-faced and pushed her another piece of paper. This letter was an altogether more abrupt affair. It was written in Biro on a piece of ordinary blue writing paper torn from a pad. It was headed 'Staithes, Yorkshire, 30 May 1962.' It read:

> Dear Augustine,
>   My private affairs remain my private affairs between me, Muriel and God. If you make any

move, I repeat, any move to my detriment in this matter, I shall inform the Arch. about you and Victor Clutton Brock and a number of other young gentlemen, giving names, dates and places.

I'll pay the window bill as I always have. I've instructed Sister Serena that you can suggest the design for one of them as you please and I'll have the other.

Yours
B.T.

PS Looking forward to being with you for the St Sylvan's festival in July.

Theodora finished reading and raised her head to look at Canon Beagle. His neck was sunk into his clerical collar, his hands folded on his chest. He glowered at Theodora. 'A pretty kettle of fish.'

'What are they exactly?'

'The Bellaire notes are both drafts, I take it. The first to Tussock was sent. Hence his reply. The second to the Archbishop wasn't.'

'And what do they show, in your view, Canon?' Theodora was cautious.

'To be blunt, they show that Bellaire liked boys too much and Tussock women.'

'Not a strong position for either to hold as priests in the Church of England.'

'Just so.'

'How did you, where did you come across these letters?'

191

Canon Beagle sighed. 'I suppose I have to admit that at one time I knew Bellaire fairly well. We shared, as I'm sure you're aware, churchmanship and the doctrine upon which that churchmanship is founded. In some ways he was a visionary, a man who realised the importance for the Church as a whole of a place like this. It is, isn't it,' he turned to Theodora for reassurance, 'paradisial?'

Theodora nodded.

'But in other ways,' Canon Beagle went on, 'he was naive. He had a quite extraordinary capacity for not seeing himself, not seeing either what he was doing or how, indeed, others would view his actions. I suppose, if I'm truthful, I would have to say he was self-deluding.'

'And the letter?' Theodora wasn't going to let the theology or the friendship bury the essential facts.

'He concealed them in his cope.' Canon Beagle almost blushed.

'Cope?'

'He designed and had made a cope for use here. I didn't think he ever actually allowed anyone else to wear it. It's really rather splendid. You should . . .' He trailed off. 'Well, anyway, I expect he felt the letters were safe there and, of course, the symbolism would appeal to him, shouldering the burden and so on.'

'You're saying you knew him, knew his mindset well enough to know where he'd hide letters of that sort?'

'Oh yes.'

'What made you suppose such letters might exist at all?'

Theodora hated the inquisitorial role. He was old enough to be her grandfather. He was an honourable man who had served, she did not doubt it, honourably in the Church she loved. But facts were facts. A woman had been killed. Wholeness, wholesomeness would not be restored whilst that was unresolved.

'I suppose one has a intuition for these things. I mean about Bellaire. About Tussock I have to say I suspected absolutely nothing. Perhaps I didn't attend to him enough to notice. I didn't care for the man. He was a frightful thruster.'

'But about Bellaire?' Theodora prompted.

'It was the last time I came. St Sylvan's Day, 25 July 1962. It was a big do. The dedication of the new windows. Bishops came. Archbishop was due to come and then cancelled. Lots of old friends. A full house. Twelve priests concelebrating. Bit of a squash in the sanctuary but we all knew what we were doing. Altar boys running about like rabbits. Enough incense to frighten off a legion of devils. Then the windows were dedicated. You've seen the windows, doubtless?'

'Yes,' said Theodora.

'And of course you've taken the inference?'

'I think so.'

Canon Beagle nodded. He could see she would.

'Didn't others see it?' Theodora was curious.

'Well, you know people are remarkably imperceptive. We are a culture unused to religious symbols. Washing powder and car advertisements have dulled our sensibilities. What would have been crystal-clear to our ancestors passed most of the congregation by.'

'But not everyone?'

'No. Clutton Brock knew.' Canon Beagle pursed his lips. 'He was a pretty young man. Hard to believe it now. Floppy hair type of thing. He'd just got engaged to Lavinia Strong.'

'And?'

'I stayed overnight. The party went on. There was a late supper and afterwards I went up to the well for a final pipe. Bellaire didn't allow smoking in the house. I came upon . . . I heard Bellaire and Clutton Brock. It was unmistakably a lovers' quarrel. I suppose about Victor's engagement. Jealousy, that sort of thing.' Canon Beagle could hardly get his words out for distaste. 'I didn't, of course, intrude or indeed stay once I'd realised.' Canon Beagle ground to a halt.

'So why didn't you do anything?'

There was a long silence. Theodora knew only too well what was going through his mind. The honour, that is, the public reputation for virtue, of the Church, the loyalty to brother priests which went far beyond their feeling for the laity, the personal factors, admiration of Bellaire, the wish to be fair to Clutton Brock, all of which would argue for keeping his own counsel.

'I was due to go back to China in a few days. I wasn't, after all, certain. You think I was wrong to leave it until now to try to find out more?'

Theodora would not judge him. She might well have done no better.

'Can your knowledge help us to clear up the present

muddle? You think there is a connection.'

'There may be. For a start, I think Ruth Swallow knew about the letters in the cope and learned from them who her father was.'

'What's your evidence?'

'The workbasket, hers. You remember she kept it on the mantelshelf in the kitchen? It had silver and gold thread in it. Not the usual material for darning Tom's socks. And there is evidence of some repair-work done on the collar of the cope.'

'Would anyone else have known that Ruth was Tussock's daughter, do you suppose? Would she have told anyone or could anyone else have found out? What I mean is, if Ruth were known to be Canon Tussock's daughter, would that make her an object of hatred to anyone, do you suppose?'

Canon Beagle considered, then he said, 'I believe Clutton Brock is a solicitor.'

Theodora turned this one over. 'Could he have got at the contents of the will?'

'I have no means of knowing.'

Theodora thought of her godmother and the lawyers in Harrogate and the phone box. She remembered too how the phone box had been occupied by Clutton Brock the first evening of their stay. She said with regret. 'I think it's just possible I might be able to find out. But I can't see why anyone who wasn't mad should want to kill Ruth just because she was Tussock's daughter.'

Canon Beagle carefully gathered up the letters from the table and placed them in order before replying. Then he glanced at Theodora. 'I think,' he said slowly, 'Clutton Brock . . . both the Clutton Brocks are mad. They torment each other. There's no health in either of them.' He went on with a rush. 'I heard . . . My room is below theirs and we're all sleeping with our windows open in this heat. The skull business. *He* said, "You're so theatrical" and *she* said, "You never seem to notice what I say. I thought you might take my meaning if it were acted out, in concrete, in bone. Bone for a bonehead." And he said "If I wake up with a nail in my forehead people will know where to come looking." And she said "Just keep your hands off the Tussock boy, that's all. I thought you came here to exorcise your ghosts not start a new generation of them."' Canon Beagle stopped. He'd found his recital a strain. He leaned back in his wheelchair.

Theodora considered his words. 'You mean Mrs Clutton Brock set up the skull thing for her husband's benefit?'

'I took her to mean that.'

'Poor woman. Did she really think Victor had his sights set on Guy?'

'I suppose a lifetime of dealing with Clutton Brock would give her that sort of intuition.'

Theodora nodded. She remembered Clutton Brock helping to steady Guy's bike on that first day before they walked down to the house. 'But she couldn't also have walked in Bellaire's cope. She was in the chapel at the time.'

'Oh no.' Canon Beagle was dismissive as one who had

worked that one out long ago. 'That could only have been Guy.'

'Why on earth . . .?'

'Bellaire's mantle falls on Guy.'

Theodora thought that was rather clever of Canon Beagle. It was just the sort of jokey way Guy might think. All this symbol-rattling would fit in with Guy's clerical family and upbringing but also turn it on its head. 'Guy's phone call to me suggested that *he* thought that the nail in the skull was a death threat.'

'Why should he think that?'

'Guy thinks, if I understand him correctly,' Theodora said, 'that there is someone here who knows the contents of the last will and testament of Canon Tussock, and who is absolutely determined that the Tussock money should go to the foundation and not to any of the Tussock descendants.'

'But both Ruth and Guy are Tussock descendants.'

'Yes, they are,' said Theodora. 'I really think I must get to a phone. Again.'

CHAPTER TWELVE

Travellers

The travellers spilled out over the countryside. Their ancient vans of composite or unknown makes revved and coughed their way slowly through the narrow lanes leading to St Sylvan's. Some came with oddly shaped horses attended by lean muscular dogs of a working variety and hoards of unbiddable children. Large women who resembled the horses and small wiry men like the dogs kept the vehicles moving. Intractable, unstoppable they flowed across the landscape, some using highways, some following forest tracks known only to themselves. Every now and again they would pull up and, in small huddles, kindle fires. They cooked and ate from communal pots. They fed each other's children and dogs, turned their horses loose amongst the hedgerows then set to the ritualised business of buying and selling. Stringed instruments vied with transistors. Goats and hens milled around amongst the wheels and the fires.

'The social mix is tremendous,' said Inspector Bottomley, scanning the horde from the police car stationed on the ridge above the valley. She had spent Thursday morning going from van to van, inquiring for Guy without success. But it had been an interesting experience, she had to admit. 'I met a man who used to teach geography at Harrow doing a deal with another man who I swear couldn't write. Though clearly he could count.'

'Pity they can't do an honest day's work,' said Luff.

'It makes for variety. You wouldn't want us all in uniform, would you, Sergeant?'

'Just an outsized slice of litter and chaos. Can't think why Broads don't object. I would.'

'It's traditional at this time of year. Anyway, it's Broads' land and if they don't object, there's nowt much we can do about it. And they'll be gone day after tomorrow, after the saint's day.'

'Can't be soon enough.'

'Keep your eye on the job. What we want is young Tussock.'

'And you reckon he might be with the ex-ambulance with a dragon on its back? Shouldn't wonder if there weren't more than one of those in a mob like this.'

'Ought to have invited the Bishop up for identification purposes.'

Luff grinned. ' "There you will find your killers, Inspector." ' He mimicked the Bishop's plummy accents.

'Down there,' said Inspector Bottomley suddenly passing the glasses to Luff. 'Coming down from behind Broadcourt.'

'Could be.'

'Right, look sharp, Sergeant.'

Mrs Lemming, sitting under the mulberry tree in the garden of the guest-house in the middle of the afternoon, stringing beans for supper, leaned forwards towards Mrs Clutton Brock and said confidentially, 'I hear they've released Tom Bough without charging him.'

Mrs Clutton Brock continued to peel potatoes. 'They couldn't have had much of a case against him.'

'I thought your husband said he saw him leave the garden about a quarter to five and move off towards the pool?'

'We were busy practising at the time. He may have been mistaken.'

'Wouldn't it have been better to have said so to the police when they questioned you the first time round?'

'I rather feel it's for the police to sort these things out.'

Mrs Lemming was scandalised by such casualness. 'But if Tom didn't kill Ruth Swallow, who did?'

Mrs Clutton Brock raised her head from her potato-peeling, looked Mrs Lemming full in the eye and said, 'Your guess is as good as mine.'

Mrs Lemming felt her efforts were not producing the effect she wanted. 'I also hear,' she upped her stake, 'that Canon Tussock's money will come to Guy Tussock and Angus hopes he will donate a bit to the foundation to keep it going instead of becoming a heritage centre. I heard Miss Braithwaite tell Angus.'

'They'll have to find him first.' Mrs Clutton Brock was curt. 'Then he'll have to prove he didn't kill Ruth.'

'You don't think he's been murdered too, do you?'

Mrs Clutton Brock had had enough. She took her peeler and went into the kitchen. For a moment she stood irresolute and then turned towards the dining-room where she expected to find Theodora laying the table. She felt the time had come. She put her head round the door. The room was empty. Reluctantly she began to mount the stairs to where she knew her husband would be waiting.

The track was steeper than Theodora remembered it. At one point it divided and she hesitated. Then she noticed the trail of oil in the grass and flattened turf. Further on she saw a couple of empty lager cans of recent date and thus encouraged pressed on. She was sweating with the effort. She'd missed lunch and swung off down to the village to the phone booth.

It had taken time. A large woman with two infants in a pushchair was making a long relaxed call which involved much laughter and many a false hope raised before she relinquished the instrument. Theodora had got hold of Broadbent and Helliwell and after much toing and froing ('the senior partner is out to lunch'), she'd elicited the fact that as far as they knew, no one had made any inquiries about the content of the Tussock will except the grandson Guy. Theodora didn't know whether she was glad or sorry at the information. If Clutton Brock didn't know about Ruth's parentage did this mean that he had no motive for murder? If he had known, it was just conceivable he was mad enough to want to destroy a descendant of Tussock as the enemy of his friend Bellaire. Or else perhaps he felt so strongly about the need to keep St Sylvan's going that financing it through the killing of the main legatee was a feasible option for him. But if neither of these held, then it was difficult to see why Clutton Brock should want to kill Ruth Swallow. So, Theodora admitted reluctantly, that left Guy.

In the far distance she could hear every now and then a burst of music or the cries of children and animals. Then the trees closed in again and the sound disappeared. She looked at her watch. It was six p.m. She really ought to be at St Sylvan's in the kitchen helping with the supper preparations. Angus had once more expressed his thanks to the 'women folk' (his words) for helping out in the kitchen. But his promise to get help from the village had come to nothing. The women's retreat was therefore one of perpetual meal provision. For the gargantuan preparations necessary to feed the guests on Friday after the festal Eucharist for St Sylvan's Day, however, he had secured Mrs Turk, he assured them triumphantly. 'She's a considerable woman,' he said in Scottish. It seemed, thought Theodora, to be the locally agreed description of Mrs T.

Theodora had embarked on her hunt for Guy, weighed down with guilt at proper work neglected in order to chase chimeras. Why had she not been content to let Inspector Bottomley do the hunting? She did rather fear that something very like professional rivalry might be her motive, which was ridiculous. She was a deacon not a sleuth. But then, she had to admit, she liked Guy. She desperately did not want him to be schizophrenic or deranged in some way enough to have been responsible for killing a fellow human being. These had been the impulses which had driven her up and down the lanes of St Sylvan's all afternoon inquiring for 'A young man with a yellow mountain bike.' She'd met much civility and genuine interest. 'Lost your lover, dearie?' was the worst she had had to cope with. But no one had any news of him. Finally she'd had a brainwave.

She pressed on up the track. The trees thinned and parted. She rounded the bend and there before her in the clearing was Bob Bough's singular cottage. Parked beside it was a large dignified-looking ambulance with a dragon painted on its back doors. Grouped round it she could see Bob Bough talking to a man in a brown gaberdine, his hair gathered in the nape of his neck in a neat queue. Sitting on the back step of the vehicle was Guy, eating a sandwich and stroking an interested-looking Jack Russell.

'Guy.'

Guy did his imitation of a vole, jumped visibly and looked as though he might bolt back into the van. Then he recognised Theodora.

'Hi. Nice to see you. Have a sandwich.'

Theodora looked at it but in spite of her lack of lunch decided against it.

'Guy, you really need to see the . . .'

Even as she spoke there was a clamour of dogs barking, horns blaring, children screaming, engines revving and amongst it all the alien, unmistakable sound of a police siren. Damn, thought Theodora, damn, damn, damn.

Inspector Bottomley's figure could be seen standing beside one of the three (how on earth had they got three into the forest?) police cars. Theodora swam through the sea of children and dogs. 'Couldn't we . . .?' she began.

Frederika Bottomley turned a sisterly face towards her. 'Sorry, love,' she said with genuine regret. 'We have our rule book, just like you've got yours. Got to have this lot for questioning and it's really much more sensible to do that somewhere quiet like Wormald police station.'

There was practically no one for supper. Angus had sent his apologies. He had a sermon to prepare for tomorrow. Guy was, of course, otherwise engaged. Neither of the Clutton Brocks put in an appearance. Canon Beagle said grace and Theodora and Mrs Lemming avoided each other's eye across the table during the silent meal. Never had Theodora found silence so little comfort. She badly wanted to discuss matters with someone sane and rational. For the first time for three days she thought of Geoffrey. She was almost minded to try and ring him this evening. But the idea of making another trek to the phone booth was too much for her, and then, she reflected, having lasted out this far it would be a pity to give way to temptation. She planned instead to give herself the pleasure of an evening meditation by the well.

As soon as Canon Beagle had said the concluding

grace she cleared the table as fast as only an ex-English girls' boarding school prefect could and washed up in the empty kitchen. Mrs Lemming did not mind preparing meals, Theodora noticed, but she was less persevering at finishing things afterwards. The clock's ticking was her only company. As she worked equanimity returned. Her thinking became more orderly and she felt impatience slipping away.

It was just a matter of getting things in the right order, she told herself as she stepped out into the garden and followed the path towards the well. The sun was beginning to set and the smells of evening were making themselves felt. There was a watery smell of moss on boulders and the dry incense of leaves recently fallen to the ground and crushed underfoot. It was possible for a moment to feel autumn and the end of summer, Theodora reflected. The weather too was beginning to change. It was cooler with a light breeze and an accumulation of clouds on the horizon. The last few steps up to the edge of the terrace round the well were wet and slippery. She negotiated them with care. Once on the terrace she stopped to take off her sandals and walked slowly and barefooted towards the deer plaque. The shadow of the ilex enclosed her.

She tried to give herself entirely to the moment, to empty her mind of everything except the beauty of the place and its consoling silence. But thoughts darted in and out of her mind like unruly fish. Of course, if the money from Tussock were to go to Guy in the event of Ruth's death, then the case for Guy having a powerful motive for wanting Ruth dead was, as Canon Beagle implied, a perfectly reasonable one. And Guy *was* an oddity, he was jokey, and unpredictable. He had known about and indeed pointed her in the direction of the will. Why had he done that, if he were guilty?

Theodora paced slowly round the edge of the well. The shadows of clouds scudded across the surface of the water. She watched the reflection of the ilex darken. It would be so easy to be hypnotised by the play of light and dark. The water rippled and mantled in a sudden breeze. What did it taste like? she wondered idly. She'd never got round to finding out. She knelt down and cupped her hands. The sound of the rock descending from a height caught her ear even as she felt the blow on the back of her head. In the far distance, as it seemed, she heard a man's voice shouting. The words she heard were 'Women pollute the sanctuary.'

'It was really very fortunate the police let Tom Bough go,' said Miss Broad to Mrs Lemming as she sliced and buttered scones on the kitchen table, in one fluent movement, 'Otherwise Theodora would have undoubtedly been killed.'

'How did Tom know to be there?' enquired Mrs Lemming.

'The police let out that it was Clutton Brock who'd said he'd seen him going up to the pool. Well, Tom knew he hadn't been so he might be lying in other matters. So he thought he'd just come back and prowl round a bit.'

'Did he know Clutton Brock was barking mad, do you suppose?'

'Well,' Miss Broad's voice was hushed, 'we none of us knew that. After all, to feel so strongly about women or place.'

'But they do, they do. Or some of them do. My own husband talks about "man being the head of woman" and it not being appropriate for women to do anything very much, as far as I can make out.'

'It goes very deep,' Miss Broad agreed. 'We are,' she held up her bread knife, 'we are a sort of pollution, a walking blasphemy. Women in the wrong place. It must have been torture for him to watch Theodora serving in the chapel at the Eucharist day after day.'

'Well, at least we're in the right place now. I don't notice anyone queuing up to usurp this ministry.' Mrs Lemming transferred her skills to cutting and arranging potted-meat sandwiches.

'And he really thought Ruth was Theodora?'

'I think the mentally deranged really do not physically see as clearly as the rest of us. It impairs all the faculties. It's both cause and result of their disease.' Mrs Lemming was knowledgeable.

'They are quite like each other. Same age and colouring. Same height. And, of course, this habit the young have of dressing in denim all the time. It would be hard to tell t'other from which from behind in the shade of the ilex,' Miss Broad agreed.

'I do feel for Lavinia,' Mrs Lemming murmured, changing from potted meat to tomato.

'Well, she married him,' said Miss Broad from her comfortable spinsterhood.

'We don't always know how it will turn out,' said Mrs Lemming, married to Norman in Tunbridge Wells.

'Can I keep the skull?' Guy asked Angus as he helped him to polish the brass alter candlesticks in readiness for the morrow. Guy had turned up for luncheon and showed every sign of a healthy appetite. The insulting windows of the chapel allowed the afternoon light to fall on the two of them as they sat in a pew in the choir and swapped Brasso and rags.

Angus felt he had had quite enough of Guy. Then he remembered the will and his real gratitude. 'Aye. If it'd please you.'

'Whose is it?' Guy enquired.

'It's no real. It's plastic. It used to be in Augustine's study. Augustine had a theatrical liking for such *memento mori*. Later it went into the vestry where, I expect, Mrs Clutton Brock picked it up.'

'But the nail's real.' Guy was anxious for reality.

'Oh aye, real enough.'

'And she put it there to warn her husband?'

'He was one of Augustine's young men.' Angus was dour.

'And she really thought the appalling Victor had designs on me?'

'She feared the atmosphere, the ghosts of the place. It was a shot across the bows.'

'I don't think I'm that way inclined,' Guy giggled nervously. 'I haven't really found out yet.'

'Ye'd do well to fast and pray,' said Angus severely. 'It's no a matter for joking. I hope you dinna want to keep the cope?'

'It's pretty sumptuous, isn't it? I wouldn't mind.'

CHAPTER THIRTEEN

St Sylvan's Day

'The end of the pilgrimage is the end of life,' said Angus. He glanced along the faces in the front row. They were mostly very senior clergy not in their first youth. Not a collection of alert intelligences, he would have to admit, and drowsy after the exertions of the previous couple of hours. They'd be wanting their tea no doubt.

Bishop Peake was centre stage, his face set and angry from his encounter with Guy Tussock. He couldn't remember when he'd had so unsatisfactory a conversation with anyone. The youth simply didn't seem to realise how very senior he was. He'd told the boy, 'It is not the wish of the senior clergy of this diocese that St Sylvan's should continue in its present form. We have agreed to sell to Modern Heritage—' Guy hadn't bothered to wait for him to finish his sentence. 'Grandad's millions are going to St Sylvan's Trust. If they've got the dosh, you can't sell them up. The lawyers say so. Grandad liked the place. I like the place. Nothing on earth would make me turn parson. Actually,' he'd leaned close to the Bishop and said confidentially, 'actually I think Buddhism has it over Christianity every time. I'm practising like mad. You should see my lotus.' The Bishop had blanched. 'We shall have to see about that,' he'd said. Those who knew Francis Peake well could have told Guy that the Bishop only used that form of words when he knew he was beaten.

Guy looked round the assembly. Angus was preaching from below the deer plaque. They'd had their Eucharist in the chapel and then processed to the well, swinging their incense, the cross guiding them. They were beautifully turned out, he had to admit. Angus's own church choir had made a good noise. The Bishop had celebrated clad in Augustine's cope. The white silk hounds leaped up his back ever stretching for the golden head of the deer. Guy wondered what they'd got for tea. Religion always made him hungry.

Mrs Turk, in the back row, thought of Ruth. The girl hadn't *done* much in her life but she had *been* someone. She'd shown quality. She was a proper offspring of the Turks. Someone to be proud of. They'd not always seen eye to eye, she and her niece, but they'd known each other's worth. Let's hope it won't all be for nothing, Mrs Turk thought. She cast her eye over the assembly, counted heads and mentally calculated sausage roll numbers. Just enough, she reckoned, and first-class too. Quite like old times. She enjoyed a get together, all sorts mixing and eating companionably. She wondered what Inspector Bottomley, three places to her left, made of it all. Not a local family, the Bottomleys. Still, she was very welcome for the festival.

'If our pilgrimage does not change us,' Angus was saying, 'if we do not learn to *want* to be different and learn *how* to be different, then that pilgrimage has been in vain.'

Mrs Lemming in the second row, thought, I'm bad for Norman. I make myself a victim and so I make him a bully. In future he will have to do with less of me. I shall enrol at Tunbridge Wells Tech for an art course. I've always fancied ceramics. And next year I'll bring Norman along here too and see if he can't change a bit as well. The resolution pleased her so much that she turned and smiled at Canon Beagle parked next to her in his wheelchair.

Canon Beagle turned his head stiffly towards her and smiled back. She wasn't a bad-looking woman when she smiled. He felt the joints in his shoulders twinge at the strain. The arthritis was gaining, no doubt about that. Soon he'd be, he had to admit it, completely dependent on others. Well, it was as good a preparation for death as possible. It was a pity he was leaving the church in such a messy state. But he was sure he'd done his bit. He was sure that Providence would prosper the work of his hand. It wouldn't, it couldn't all be in vain.

'It seems to be a paradox of Christian pilgrimage that those who stand still go furthest in their journey,' Angus was saying. ' "*Qui restitit ei pax datur*" is written above us.' Angus was winding up for his peroration. 'It is self-knowledge which we seek and self-knowledge which, if we courageously allow it, will lead us on from truth to truth until we reach the last Truth of all, God, the fountain of all peace.'

He's going above their heads, thought Martha Broad. She was well back in the body of the congregation. The chapel in which they had worshipped was on land the gift of her family. She, though newly in priests' orders, had not been invited to concelebrate. She lifted her eyes to the hills. On each one, there could be seen the blue smoke of fires kindled by the travellers encamped like the Pictish hordes of St Sylvan's own day. The smell of chickens and rabbits mixed with that of nut roast. They had come, as she had seen them do year after year since she was a girl, driving their goats and chickens in front of them, with their scrawny horses unused to the bit and their large women sunk in their pregnancies. Why on earth do they come? What had Christianity to say to them? Martha Broad wondered. Every now and again a burst of shouting or music or dogs barking would puncture the air and remind the pious assembly below that theirs was not the only society. There were other possibilities. Fewer possessions, less oppression, less hierarchy, less struggle, less unkindness, the Reverend the Honourable Martha Broad thought, and for a moment was almost tempted. She looked across at Theodora, sitting further down the same row, her head swathed in bandages. Her pilgrimage will be longer than mine, she thought. Will it get any better for her?

AN ECCLESIASTICAL WHODUNNIT

CLERICAL ERRORS

D. M. Greenwood

In the shadow of honey-coloured Medewich Cathedral, amidst the perfect lawns of the Cathedral Close, the diocesan office of St Manicus should have been a peaceful if not an especially exciting place for nineteen-year-old Julia Smith to start her first job. Yet she has been in its precincts for less than an hour when she stumbles on a horror of Biblical proportions – a severed head in the Cathedral font.

And she has worked for the suave Canon Wheeler for less than a day when she realises that the Dean and Chapter is as riven by rivalry, ambition and petty jealousy as the court of any Renaissance prelate. In this jungle of intrigue a young deaconess, Theodora Braithwaite, stands out as a lone pillar of common sense. Taciturn but kindly, she takes Julia under her wing, and with the assistance of Ian Caretaker – a young man who hates Canon Wheeler as much as he loves the Church – they attempt to unravel the truth behind the death of a well-meaning man, the Reverend Paul Gray, late incumbent of Markham cum Cumbermound.

FICTION / CRIME 0 7472 3582 1

A selection of bestsellers from Headline